PEACEMAKER
RAWHIDE

PEACEMAKER
RAWHIDE

•

CLIFFORD BLAIR

AVALON BOOKS
THOMAS BOUREGY AND COMPANY, INC.
401 LAFAYETTE STREET
NEW YORK, NEW YORK 10003

PRINTED IN THE UNITED STATES OF AMERICA
ON ACID-FREE PAPER
BY HADDON CRAFTSMEN, BLOOMSBURG, PENNSYLVANIA

With love,
to Rachel,
my granddaughter,
who has brightened
our lives.

Chapter One

James Stark heard the sudden boom of gunfire and reined his big sorrel to a sharp stop. Frowning, he cocked his head to listen, squinting at the small range of hills looming in front of him. Sounds as though somebody had bought themselves a passel of trouble up there, he reflected grimly.

After a moment he swung the sorrel off the trail onto the prairie. Trouble was his business, but only a tenderfoot would ride blind into a shooting scrap. He was no tenderfoot.

Still, a sudden prickling of urgency stirred him, and he put Red into a lope, circling wide to head into the hills. The dense buffalo grass, made dry by the coolness of late fall, broke with brittle crispness beneath the sorrel's hooves.

Two parties were trading shots, he calculated as he drew nearer. The rapid firing of two or three repeating rifles sounded sharply in the heights. From the far side of the hills came the more muffled return fire of a handgun and

1

a single-shot rifle. Stark felt the muscles of his face tighten. This fracas had all the earmarks of a bushwhacking gone bad, one that had given the intended victims a chance to fight back, even though the odds, and the firepower, were clearly against them.

Automatically Stark's hand dropped to check his own firepower. His fingertips brushed the butt of the Colt .45 Peacemaker holstered at his hip, touched the hilt of the custom bowie knife, then flicked to the double-action Marlin .38 hideout gun sheathed behind his cartridge belt at the small of his back. Finally they came lightly to rest on the stock of the ten-gauge Winchester 1887 lever-action shotgun he generally favored over a rifle. The feel of the smooth wood touched him with a reassuring confidence.

Movement on a scrub-covered grade caught his eye. ''Whoa, Red,'' he muttered, and eased the stallion to a halt in a narrow defile which snaked up into the hills.

Deftly he unshipped his fine German field glasses and lifted them to his eyes. Red stood as motionless as one of the stony outcroppings studding the hillsides. The pale midday sun was high enough so that Stark didn't need to worry about a betraying reflection from the lenses. Besides, he figured, the drygulchers had other things on their minds than looking for any hostile interlopers in their affairs.

It took a moment for him to catch the rifle-toting figure of a man scrambling up a rocky bluff toward a higher summit. Looking for a better vantage point, Stark mused. The yahoo's face was in shadow, but his crisscrossed pistol belts marked him as a hard case rather than some stray cowpoke.

Stark lowered the glasses just a bit and studied the hill adjacent to the summit. Sure enough, spaced along its crest, he spotted first the powder smoke, then the kneeling figures of two more bushwhackers. Their rifles spoke in a steady covering fire directed down at the trail on the far side of

the hill. Whoever they'd targeted was likely pinned down
and helpless to do more than throw an occasional shot in
return. There was no immediate sign of the bushwhackers'
horses. Probably they were concealed nearby.

Stark took a moment longer to study the terrain below
the lone rifleman. A good rider could crest the hill without
too much effort, but, unless he was careful, he'd be in plain
sight for a good stretch. That could mean trouble if any of
the drygulchers happened to glance over his shoulder.

Stark shoved the field glasses into his saddlebag. He was
tempted to cut loose on the ambushers from where he sat
his horse. He didn't doubt he could send them hightailing
from their current positions, and even do a lot more to them
if he had a mind to. But a spark of caution stayed his hand.

It was just possible this sorry-looking crew had a legit-
imate reason for throwing lead at whoever they had cornered on the far side of the hill. Not likely, but possible.
They didn't have the cut of lawmen—bounty hunters,
maybe—but their prey could be some notorious lawbreak-
ers who were well deserving of this type of trap.

Men of the lawless brand rode free as mustangs in parts
of Oklahoma Territory and the neighboring Indian lands. It
took a hardy breed to track them down. Stark himself was
a pretty fair example of that. Returning to the territorial
capital of Guthrie from a cattle-rustling investigation, he
didn't look too reputable himself at the moment.

In any event, the quarry almost certainly didn't have
much time left. Once the rifleman reached a suitable vantage point the uneven duel would be quickly over.

Stark loosened the shotgun in its scabbard and heeled
Red on up the narrow defile. In moments he was out of
sight of the drygulchers, although the echoing exchange of
gunfire still came clearly to his ears. The draw angled in
the direction he wanted to go, and he kept Red in its cover
until it petered out in a thicket of brush. He sent Red bull-

ing through the undergrowth, still unable to see any of the gunmen.

Swiftly he worked his way upward toward the summit of the hill. Red's hooves clattered and slipped over a steep stretch of loose talus, and Stark finally reined him to a halt in the cover of a towering boulder. Sweat trickled down Stark's neck. The stone and brush of the hills trapped the meager warmth of the sun, and those last few yards on the grade he'd been flat out in the open.

Shotgun in his fist, he swung one leg over and slid lightly out of the saddle. His Apache moccasins would've made traveling afoot easier and quieter, but he didn't reckon he could take time to don them. In the minutes he had spent reaching this spot, the lone bushwhacker had probably found a site to suit his lethal purposes. As if to confirm his guess, a shot rang out from the summit above him.

Stark legged it up the grade, crouching to offset its steepness and to present as small a target as possible. By habit he stayed to the cover of brush and boulders wherever he could.

Another shot came from above. The loner was either finishing his work or getting his range, Stark calculated bleakly. But the rifle's report and its puff of powder smoke let him spot its owner's position. The drygulcher had gone to ground in a jumble of boulders skirted by a fringe of brush. Stark breathed out hard through his nostrils. This particular drygulcher was about to have the tables turned on him.

Like a stalking puma, Stark catfooted upwards. The other bushwhackers were still throwing lead, but they'd slacked off some, probably satisfied to let their pard complete their ugly job.

Crouched behind an outcropping of stone on a shoulder just below his prey's site, Stark peered down toward the trail and got his first glimpse of the trio's elusive targets.

Both of his big fists tightened, then shifted over the smooth wood and metal of the shotgun.

A dead horse sprawled across the grassy ruts of the trail. In a shallow gully beyond the carcass, a pair of tow-haired figures were hunkered down low. Stark couldn't see much, but the pair's near identical palomino shade of hair made him think automatically of offspring of the same parents. And the long tresses of the more slender figure left no doubt as to its gender. One of the helpless pair was a female, and, from their size, neither of them were much more than kids.

As Stark stared, dumbstruck, the blond young man raised slightly to send a rifle slug up the hill. Not to be outdone, his companion cut loose with a pistol a moment later. Instantly both of them flattened themselves as a flurry of fire from the two lower riflemen answered them. Stark saw bullets kick up dust along the lip of the gully, heard one bounce screaming off of stone.

The two of them were putting up a game fight, sure enough. The gully seemed to offer barely adequate cover against the riflemen sniping at them. But the pair would be nothing more than shooting-gallery targets for the third bushwhacker.

And even now he probably had found his range and was drawing a final bead on them.

In a swift, silent rush, Stark went up the last few yards, and halted, crouching. Ten feet distant, through a screen of growth, he saw the kneeling figure of the bushwhacker. The butt of his rifle was settled snugly against his shoulder as he took aim down its barrel. Stark could see the edge of an ugly grin splitting his black-whiskered face.

The careful way to play this was to throw down on him from cover and order him to drop his rifle without ever giving him a chance to make a play of his own. Stark wasn't feeling careful. Anger roiled in him. Shotgun tilted skyward, he stepped through the brush and into the open.

"Nice day for a bushwhacking," he growled.

The hard case jerked in startlement. His coarse, stubbled face turned sharply toward Stark.

"Right there, hero," Stark advised coldly.

He watched the bushwhacker weighing it, gauging his chances. He wasn't under a dead drop; the shotgun's barrel was pointed straight up. If he already had a shell chambered in the rifle, which was likely, then, provided he was fast enough, he just might pivot and get off a shot before Stark could level the shotgun and fire.

It was a chance the bushwhacker chose to take. In a single surge of motion and effort, he twisted at the waist, the rifle barrel swinging in an arc toward Stark's looming figure.

The arc was never completed. One-handed, Stark tipped the shotgun level and pulled the trigger. He didn't need to work the lever. The bushwhacker wasn't the only one who already had a shell chambered. Even with his arm braced against his body, the recoil jolted Stark to the roots of his teeth. At point-blank range, the solid load—a miniature cannonball—smashed the drygulcher flat. His rifle clattered unfired from his lifeless hands.

"Not such a nice day after all," Stark muttered with grim satisfaction. Some men just flat needed killing. This fellow had been one.

Unthinkingly, he thumbed a shell from one of his criss-cross bandoleers and slid it into the shotgun to replace the empty. It was another solid load; he alternated those with .00 buckshot. Reloaded, he stepped forward to confirm the kill.

As he moved, a rifle bullet sang past his ear. He dropped flat and made three scrambling yards on knees and elbows before stopping. He knew what had happened. One of his victim's compadres had spotted him and fired upslope. Twisting on his belly, Stark peered over a low ridge.

Not much more than a pair of seconds had passed. Just enough time for the shooter to be lowering his rifle, unsure whether or not he'd scored a hit. Stark caught the dull glint of metal below the cloud of powder smoke that hovered over a tiny natural fortress of brush and stone.

He barely bothered to aim. Rapid-fire, working the lever and pulling the trigger, he pumped three loads into the fortress. Buckshot, solid, then buckshot again, leaving the final load for backup if needed. The butt of the shotgun punched his shoulder like a prizefighter's driving fist. Through the smoke he saw leaves and branches shredded, and rocks chipped beneath the fusillade. Over the ringing in his ears he heard a man cry out. The rifle barrel disappeared.

Stark rolled twice sideways. The drygulcher in the fortress might or might not be out of action, but there was a third enemy still lurking somewhere down there. Again he reloaded, surveying the terrain with narrowed eyes, sparing an occasional glance at the fortress. No sound or movement from there. Stark wondered remotely what the pair of intended victims were making of his taking a hand in the affair.

Warily he snaked his way upward past the vantage point the lone drygulcher had chosen. He was careful not to skyline himself to the pair in the gully. Be a fine thing to get picked off by one of them, he reflected wryly.

"Ben? You hit? Hank? What happened? Did he get you?" a man's voice bounced from the hillside.

"They're both dead!" Stark shouted. "You're next!" He wriggled higher. The echoes had kept him from pinpointing the third killer's location. He had to figure the drygulcher was also changing position after having shouted his queries. Likely he had played such a stalking game before.

Just like Stark.

"Who are you?" the drygulcher's voice rang out again.

Yeah, he'd moved all right, Stark concluded. "Name's James Stark!" he shouted in answer.

A moment of stunned silence. "Why are you butting in on this?" a hollered query came then.

"Just passing through! Didn't want to miss the fun!"

Stark thought he had him located now, and the reverse was probably true as well. He drove a solid load at a rocky outcropping on the crest of the neighboring hill, then flicked a fist-sized stone clattering downslope. He hoped the combination—gunshot, then sound of movement—would bait the ambusher into view, allowing for a shot.

The hombre was fast. Almost before Stark could get both hands back on the shotgun, the head and upper body of the drygulcher appeared from the midst of the outcropping. His rifle tracked the course of the stone. He went rigid in surprise at not finding a target in his sights. Stark, with a target in his own sights, sent a load of buckshot screaming down that way. With a solid slug he might've missed, but with the spreading blast of buckshot there wasn't much likelihood of it.

The bushwhacker reeled from the shelter of the outcropping and plunged down the hill on the far side in a sliding fall. His limp form came to rest in a shallow depression not far above the trail.

Hoofbeats brought Stark's head around. A mounted figure, hunched awkwardly in the saddle, was hightailing it out on the flatlands away from the hills. Somehow the wounded hard case in the rock fortress had managed to secure one of the trio's horses and put it to good use.

Stark lifted his shotgun, then lowered it slowly. Despite the ploy he'd used on the first bushwhacker, he had no stomach for killing men when it didn't have to be done.

Besides, his arm and shoulder still ached brutally from his fool stunt of firing the shotgun one-handed.

He turned away as the figure of the fleeing drygulcher grew smaller. "Hold your fire!" he called. "I'm coming down!"

"Come ahead!"

He paused in his descent only long enough to confirm the death of the third bushwhacker. Several of the heavy buckshot pellets had caught him. Stark didn't count how many; they'd been enough to do the job.

As he reached the trail at the foot of the hill he saw the tow-headed pair emerging warily from the draw which had sheltered them. Up close, the notion that they were kin was undeniable. Brother and sister, he'd bet. They shared the same regular features—firm and handsome on him, softer and very pretty on her. Even covered in dust, weary from a gun battle, and clad in faded work clothes, they made a nice-looking pair. The pride and joy of some father and mother, no doubt.

Stark pegged the young man as being the older by maybe a year. Probably eighteen or so, with husky build. His sis was still not quite yet a woman, although the man's clothes she wore left no doubt of her femininity.

She held back, busying herself in trying to brush the red dust from her clothing. The young man came forward, clamping a battered slouch hat down on his unruly hair.

"You sure saved our bacon," he acknowledged seriously. "Did I hear you right? You're James Stark, the Peacemaker?"

Peacemaker. It was the nickname commonly given to Colt six-shooters like he carried, and the name under which he'd chosen to operate his business as a professional troubleshooter: Peacemaker for Hire.

Peacemaker, troubleshooter; there'd been other names for the trades he'd followed over the years: lawman, bounty hunter, railroad detective, private investigator, shotgun guard, prizefighter. All those things and more in his background had led him to the trail he rode now.

"Yeah, I'm James Stark," he answered. The girl, he noted, had gone to kneel sadly by the dead horse. She touched its head gently. "Where you folks headed?" Stark asked the young man.

"Guthrie," the reply came readily enough. "We're on our way there to meet with a lawyer. Hoping we can get in to see her tomorrow."

"Her?" Stark said with a growing suspicion.

A quick nod. "A lady lawyer. Ain't that the blamedest thing? But Pa swore by her. Told us if anything ever happened, to make tracks straight to her. Her's name's Prudence McKay. You ever heard of her?"

"I reckon you could say that," Stark told him.

The youngster's expression grew puzzled at the wry tone of his voice.

Chapter Two

"Hello, Mr. Stark. I'm glad you got my message and were able to come. I believe you met my clients on the trail yesterday."

Prudence McKay was being unexpectedly formal as she ushered Stark into her office. Probably something to do with having to behave like a lawyer in front of her clients, Stark figured. "Why, I believe I did, Miss McKay," he said with a sardonic twang to his voice, and had the satisfaction of seeing her pretty features color fetchingly.

As usual, almost everything about her was fetching. Even dressed for the office in a dark modest dress, her petite figure was thoroughly feminine. As she stepped aside to let him pass, he caught a faint sweet scent from her. The top of her head was a bit below his shoulder. Her brunet hair was worn up in a neatly coiled braid. Stark had occasion to know that, when her hair was loose, it tumbled most becomingly past her slender shoulders. He also had occasion to know that she was soft and warm and light as a feather when she was in his arms on the dance floor.

Of course, he mused, reining in his thoughts, any notion of seriously paying court to her was out of the question. She was far too headstrong and independent for him to ever consider putting his brand on her permanently, even if he was ready to be roped and tied by a female.

The daughter of a Kansas judge, Prudence had attended law school at the urging of her freethinking father. Then, over his protests, had come down to the tumultuous Oklahoma Territory to make her name as an attorney. And make it she had, earning herself a reputation as an honest, savvy barrister who could hold her own in any courtroom and before any judge. Stark had seen her in action; once she had even defended him on a trumped-up charge. In a court scrap he knew he'd rather have her on his side than any other lawyer in the territory.

Her office was simply but tastefully furnished. Stacked bookcases held various legal tomes. Her framed diplomas were arranged on the wall behind her neatly kept desk. A display of brightly colored autumn leaves lent a distinctive woman's touch.

The tow-headed siblings he'd rescued on the trail were just rising from the upholstered chairs in front of the desk as Stark entered. The girl had replaced her man's garb with a plain homespun dress. In it she looked even more youthful and girlish. Her brother wore a clean shirt and denim pants. His battered slouch hat was wadded in one hand. A holstered pistol rode his hard waist.

"Brian and Brenda Langton," Prudence was going ahead with the unneeded introductions. "They're from Doaksville in Indian territory."

In truth, however, while the introductions weren't necessary, that last bit of information was new to Stark. Following his run-in with the bushwhackers the day before, he'd had little chance to learn more than their names and the fact that they hailed from the Indian lands. On the ride to Guthrie he had ranged far and wide of the trail, scouting the rolling grasslands for signs that the wounded hard case had returned with additional cohorts, or that other enemies might be stalking the young pair.

But the trip had passed uneventfully, and, late in the day, Stark had seen them to an inexpensive rooming house, then checked in at the office of U.S. Marshal Evett Nix to report the deaths of the two luckless drygulchers. In his trade, which often skirted the edge of the law, it never hurt to stay on good terms with the local peace officers.

He suspected the ambush had been more than a random attack by stickup artists, but the following morning he'd been too busy catching up on paperwork at his office to pursue his hunch. He hoped this meeting with Prudence and her new clients would open the door to some answers about the whole affair.

"Doaksville," he echoed aloud now. "Near old Fort Towson." Pretty remote even for the Indian lands, he added to himself.

Prudence stepped behind her desk as Stark settled into another client chair. She remained standing, looking lovely even in the austere business setting, Stark thought. He caught himself and scowled mentally. He was always having such fool distracting thoughts around Prudence.

He shifted to get comfortable in the chair. It appeared as though he was in for some sort of formal talk from Prudence. He wore his usual city attire of corduroy coat, white shirt, string tie, whipcord pants, and high boots. Both handguns were in place. He was no longer the disreputable gunman he'd appeared the day before. Now he was a respectable gunman.

He'd doffed his Stetson upon entering the office. He set

it aside on a small end table as Prudence picked up a sheaf of typed pages from her desk.

"Brian and Brenda's father was a client of mine," she began by way of explanation. "His name was Jacob Langton. Shortly after I opened my practice, he was in Guthrie on business and came to me to have his will drafted." She tightened her hold on the papers she held. "I prepared this for him, and he signed it. I kept a copy for my file. He was a good man," she added.

Brenda bit her lip. Brian gave a short nod of acknowledgment.

Prudence laid the will aside and picked up a single page of cheaper quality paper. Stark saw words scrawled on it in a plain bold hand. "This is an amendment to that will," she went on, "A codicil."

"Holographic one," Stark murmured.

If she was surprised at his legal knowledge, Prudence didn't let much of it show on her face. "That's right; it's handwritten. Apparently Mr. Langton wrote this himself when he was back in Doaksville. I certainly did not encourage him or advise him to do so." She paused. "Brian and Miss Brenda brought both of these documents to me. Their father passed away recently. In his codicil, he named me as executor of his estate."

Stark thought of the three hard-case bushwhackers. "How did he die?" he asked aloud.

Brian's smooth brow grew furrowed. "An accident. He fell off one of our wagons he was driving. He was the owner of B&B Freight, a freighting company."

Brenda's pretty countenance was even more troubled than her brother's, but she cut a glance at him and kept silent out of obvious deference to him.

"I'll let them tell you about some of the problems their father's company had encountered," Prudence said.

"Problems?" Stark prodded. His interest was quickening.

Brian shifted a little uneasily as if reluctant to proceed. His sister didn't look nearly so hesitant, but it was the older sibling who went ahead and spoke.

"Pa had built up a pretty good business," Brian began. "There's plenty of work for a small freight line down in our area. The railroads haven't reached that far yet."

Stark nodded his understanding. With the advent of the iron horse, the giant old-time freight companies, like that of Russell, Majors, and Waddell, had all but vanished. Their function of transporting goods of every nature throughout the sprawling nation had been taken over by the faster and less risky method of rail transport.

But no rail spurs had yet reached into remote areas such as that around Doaksville and the long abandoned Fort Towson. In such regions small freight lines still provided a major service, transporting goods and mail from the nearest railheads to local farms, ranches, and communities. But freighting was hard, unrelenting work. It said a lot about Jacob Langton that he'd made a success of such an enterprise.

"We got us a good operation; three working wagons and a crew," Brian went on. "Counting me and Sis and our hostler, we still got three mule skinners. Then some kid that's been hanging around makes a pretty good hand, I reckon."

His sister gave him a spirited glare, which he ignored.

"About a year before Pa's death, we started having trouble. Another freight line opened up in Doaksville, and the owner wanted to buy us out. Pa turned him down cold; said he'd put too much of himself into the B&B, and that he wanted to leave it to me and Brenda. That's when things started going sour. Nothing definite we could blame on anyone, you understand. Could've just been bad luck or accidents at first: broken reins, a busted wheel spoke that might've been partly sawed through, mules coming up sick or lame. Pa still wouldn't sell, and it got worse. Somebody broke into our warehouse. We had a few stray shots thrown our way, with no trace who was doing the shooting.

"We even had a couple of masked hombres hold up one of our wagons. Lost a good load of freight to them, blast their sorry hides. That made us start having to use someone to ride shotgun on each haul; cut our work force in half, what with two hands needed to make each trip." He broke off to shake his head tiredly, as though his own words had brought the full weight of their predicament down on his sturdy shoulders at last. "Now that Pa's gone, I'm not so sure how we can keep the wagons rolling. Could be, we'll have to sell out after all."

"Not to *her,* we won't!" Brenda snapped. Her blue eyes blazed fiercely.

"Her?" Stark echoed. "I thought you said the owner of the other freight line was a man."

"Originally it was," Brian explained. "Then he up and died, and his widow took over. Thanks to what he left her, she owns nigh onto half the town. Name's Norene Danner, and she's as mean as a she-wolf with scorched fur. I reckon we could've gotten along with Old Man Danner, but she's a horse of a different color."

"How'd her husband die?" Stark wondered aloud.

Brian shrugged. "Riding accident. He fell off his horse." He worked his mouth as if to rid it of a bad taste.

"You think she's behind the hoorawing your outfit's been getting?"

Brian shifted uncomfortably. "Couldn't prove nothing like that," he hedged. "But the trouble really got serious when she got her hands on the reins of Old Man Danner's holdings."

"You figure she sent those hard cases after the two of you on the trail?"

"I think she did!" Brenda chimed in before her brother could answer. "And I think she killed Dad, too!"

"Killed him how?" Stark demanded.

A look of frustration crossed her pretty features. "I don't know," she admitted reluctantly. "Brian and I both saw the tracks where it happened. Clete looked them over with us. He's our other mule skinner. It seems like Dad just fell out of the wagon while the team was ambling along at a walk. There was no sign the mules got out of control, and, anyway, Dad was as good a man with the lines and rawhide as anybody who ever sat a wagon seat." A fiery pride rang in her tone.

"What kind of injuries did he have?"

Brian took up the slack. "Neck was broke and his skull busted," he said bitterly.

"From falling off a wagon with the team moving at a walk!" Stark exclaimed. "That doesn't rightly make sense."

Brian hitched his shoulders about. "Nope, but that's still what the doc said happened. I seen Dad's body, and it looked that way to me, too."

"Who's the doc?"

"Doc Harrison, an old sawbones. He looks after men and animals, both, when they're ailing. I don't know as how he's ever had any real medical training, but he's the closest thing we got to a doctor or a vet around Doaksville."

Not much of a coroner, Stark mused. Still, it was hard even for a layman to mistake a broken neck and a crushed skull. He put the subject aside for the moment. "So you came up here to see about having Prudence—Miss Mc-Kay—probate the will?"

"Yep, that's the size of it. Dad left everything to me and

Brenda equally. We hated to leave the running of things to Clete and Josh, but we figured as how both of us needed to come.''

Brenda nodded emphatically. ''We both want Miss Mc-Kay to be the executor in keeping with Dad's wishes.''

Stark glanced at Prudence. She had remained standing behind her desk, the codicil still in her hands.

''I never asked your father to name me,'' she announced a trifle defensively. ''I don't approve of the practice some attorneys have of appointing themselves as executor in wills they draw up. It strikes me as unethical.'' She drew a solemn breath. ''But since your father did see fit to name me, and since I have the approval of you both, I'll agree to do what he asked of me. Indeed, I feel a certain obligation under the circumstances to carry out his wishes. I'm flattered that he placed such confidence in me.''

The words could've been spoken as some sort of formal argument in court, but there was no doubting the depth of her sincerity. Stark caught himself staring with rapt admiration.

''Probate is a court-supervised process of seeing to it that the provisions of a decedent's will are carried out,'' she continued. ''It is a complex and time-consuming procedure.''

Now she sounded like she was delivering a lecture to some first-year class of law students, Stark reflected sourly.

''The case will have to be heard in South McAlister,'' he broke in deliberately. ''The next session of federal court doesn't open there for a month. That means you'll have to wait at least that long to file the will.''

''Actually,'' Prudence corrected with a trace of smugness, ''I can file it immediately. But the hearing on it can't take place until after the court is in session.''

''That's Judge Shackleford's court,'' Stark said almost before she finished her statement. He was vaguely aware of the eyes of the Langton kids shifting back and forth between them with each exchange.

"That's right," Prudence smiled sweetly. "He and my father are old friends. I certainly look forward to seeing him again." She returned her attention to her clients and went on with scarcely a pause. "I asked Mr. Stark to join us today because I believe there may be some risk in you returning to Doaksville to operate the freight company before the probate is opened." She stilled their objections with a raised palm. "As the named executor, I propose that we retain Mr. Stark to accompany you to Doaksville to protect the interests of the estate, and investigate the possible sabotage of the business, at least until the estate has been formally opened under Judge Shackleford's jurisdiction. Longer, if necessary. Does that meet with your approval?"

"It would be wonderful!" Brenda exclaimed. Brian nodded hearty approval.

"Then it's settled—" Prudence broke off abruptly as she looked at Stark.

He cocked a skeptical gaze at her. "Does that mean I'd be working for you?" he drawled.

Chapter Three

"I can't believe you had us come out here to discuss this!" Prudence fumed. She and Stark were alone in the reception area of her office. "You've worked for me before!"

"We've cooperated on a case before," Stark corrected. "And I've acted as an expert witness, but I've never worked for you."

"And just what's wrong with you working for me?" Prudence flared. "Those young people need your help—our help! I thought you'd appreciate me recommending you—"

"Don't be doing me any favors," Stark cut her off with a growl. "I don't need you shilling for me." He had started this almost as a lark, but her high-handed attitude was an effective goad to his anger.

"Shilling for you?" she echoed. "Is that what you think I'm doing?" Her eyes were surprisingly bright. "You've

20

referred clients to me. Now when I try to return the favor, you act like I've insulted your mule-headed pride!''

Stark understood abruptly that he had offended her, maybe seriously, with his own attitude. Things had gotten out of hand here somewhere.

''That's just what I'd expect,'' she stormed on, ''From a—a . . .''

''Hired gun?'' Stark supplied dryly.

''Those are your words, not mine!'' she snapped.

Stark didn't remind her that once they had been her words. Remotely he wondered why he kept provoking her. She was glowering at him with fierce defiance in her moist eyes. He never could quite get his emotions corraled when he was around her.

''Simmer down,'' he made the effort just the same.

''Are you saying you won't take the job?'' she interposed sharply.

Stark wished he was back stalking the bushwhackers. Hostile rifles and six-guns he could handle.

''Just want it clear who'll be in charge,'' he said doggedly. ''I don't take kindly to following orders.''

''Meaning you'll be in charge?''

Stark hitched his shoulders in a shrug. ''Yeah, when it comes to troubleshooting.''

She put both hands on her hips and glared up at him. ''That's fine with me. You don't tell me how to handle the probate, and I won't tell you how to handle the killing!'' She broke off and bit down hard on her lower lip. Her face went pale. She opened her mouth as though to retract the words.

Piqued, Stark wouldn't let her. ''Just remember I don't work cheap,'' he said tightly before she could speak.

Color blossomed back in her cheeks. ''Don't worry, Mr. Stark. You'll be paid exactly what you're worth!''

It didn't sound as if that was very much in her opinion. She wheeled and disappeared back into her office. Stark knew better than to follow. Shaking his head, he went out into Guthrie's busy streets. He questioned grimly if this was a job he should've turned down. But Prudence had been right about one thing. Those young folks needed help, both in court and out. From the looks of it, they were going to have a steep uphill pull to keep the B&B going.

He received a terse note by messenger the following morning. Tickets had been reserved for him and Mr. and Miss Langton on the train leaving for South McAlister on the morrow. Apparently Prudence, in her new role as named executor, had decided it was worth the cost of rail passage to get him and her clients back to Doaksville as soon as possible. Grudgingly, Stark acknowledged she was likely right.

He finished catching up on correspondence and reviewing new wanted circulars, then wrote a detailed report of the investigation he'd just closed. His client had been a member of a local cattlemen's association. The regular retainer paid by the organization had covered his services in tracking down a pair of saddle tramps making a stab at cattle rustling. Cornered, they'd seemed almost relieved to surrender. With winter coming on, three squares and a bunk, even in the stony lonesome, might've been looking pretty good to them.

Stark saw to Red in the stable, then, following dinner at his hotel's dining room, returned to his office and set to inspecting and cleaning his firearms and honing the blade on his custom bowie knife.

A brisk night had fallen by the time he locked up his office and sauntered back toward his hotel. By habit, he kept his eyes moving, probing the darkness, glancing every so often over his shoulder. Wariness was bred into him after years of riding the danger trail. Trouble could be lurking even in the familiar terrain of the city. The wariness had kept him alive, that and the weapons that seemed as much a part of him now as his caution.

There'd been no further word from Prudence. He'd entertained the idea of looking her up for dinner, but had shrugged that fool notion aside almost as soon as it came to him. Just like her to make train reservations without so much as a by-your-leave. Never broke to saddle, that was her problem. But heaven pity the poor hombre who tried. He certainly wasn't angling for the job.

Early the next morning he brought Red to the depot so he could be sure arrangements had been made for hauling the big sorrel in the stock car. He needn't have bothered. Prudence had taken care of that too, he discovered, as well as providing for the remaining Langton mount to be transported.

Stark had just secured the stallion and emerged from the stock car when he spotted Brian leading the other horse through the people already beginning to bustle around the train. The youngster was garbed as he had been in Prudence's office. His slouch hat was pulled down snug against his ears. His face broke into a grin as he saw Stark.

"Morning, Mr. Stark," he greeted.

"It's Jim," Stark said absently, peering past him. He put his eyes back on the younger man. "Where's your sister?" he queried.

"Yonder, with Miss McKay." Brian jerked his head back over his shoulder.

Stark slipped by him with a nod of thanks. Toting his war bag he threaded his way through the press of people. Weatherbeaten ranchers mingled with brash drummers, harried businessmen, stoic Indians, and pompous legislators.

Stark caught a fleeting glimpse of Brenda's yellow hair. He all but ignored her as his eyes fell on Prudence's slender form beside the taller girl. Oddly, Prudence wasn't wearing her usual unassuming business attire. Rather, she sported a colorful calico dress with a lacy neckline that might've been better suited to a Saturday night church social.

She gave him a hesitant smile as he drew near, then forestalled him speaking by pressing a thick envelope on him. "I need you to do me a favor." Her tone was soft and imploring. "Please."

Stark was nonplussed. He wasn't sure if he'd been expecting a resumption of hostilities or a cold shoulder. Of a sudden he realized he hadn't even had a notion as to what he planned to say to her at this meeting.

Automatically he set his war bag on the platform beside him and reached to take the envelope. He fancied she held it a moment longer than necessary, and he felt the fleeting brush of her fingertips as she relinquished it to his grasp. Her eyes, gazing up at his face, were unreadable.

"That's Mr. Langton's will and the pleadings to start the probate," she went on in a slightly more businesslike tone before he could summon words. "I've already wired to set a hearing date. Can you file these for me in McAlister?"

He nodded. "Happy to do it," he managed, and squared his shoulders. The remote understanding came to him that he'd just been disarmed as neatly as a tenderfoot in a stage stickup. But he didn't mind.

"Thank you." Prudence drew a half step closer. Her eyes were still fixed intently on his face. He felt the familiar touch of her hand on his chest, light as a hummingbird. "Be careful," she said softly.

All of their own accord, Stark's arms started to lift to embrace her. He checked the impulse. She went very still as if in fear or anticipation; he wasn't sure which.

"Got the horse loaded," Brian announced as he came up to them. He blinked in surprise at the look his sister shot him.

Stark became aware of the crowd, of Prudence stepping

hastily back from him, her cheeks a fiery red. He'd been standing there like some moonstruck yokel, he berated himself with disgust. Good thing Prudence wasn't going along on this jaunt. With her around he sure wouldn't be able to concentrate on the business at hand. He hoped he'd have her out of his blood by the time she had to come down for the hearing on the will.

Brenda was grinning at the pair of them, and Brian wore a puzzled expression.

"I'll be in South McAlister the first day of the court docket," Prudence advised, all crisp efficiency. "Let me know if you have any trouble before then."

Stark couldn't quite catch her eye. "I'll holler if we need help," he promised laconically.

Prudence's trim shoulders stiffened ever so slightly. "Very well." The deafening blast of the train's whistle cut off anything else she had to add.

"We better move," Stark said. He tucked the envelope inside his coat and hefted his war bag. He could feel the weight of the shotgun and rifle in it. Brian handed Brenda up into the passenger car and Stark swung up after them. He hesitated for a moment, glancing back at Prudence. She gave him a small smile.

"So long." He touched his hat to her, then moved on into the narrow aisle of the car.

Brenda had apparently waited there for him. "You're sweet on her, aren't you?" she whispered with conspiratorial eagerness.

Fool girl, Stark thought. "Not hardly," he growled, and hefted the war bag to stow it in the overhead rack.

More folks had disembarked from the train than had gotten on it. Stark and the youngsters got settled at the back of the car where Stark could keep an eye on the few other travelers who shared it with them. He was across the aisle from Brian. Beside her brother, Brenda was peering out the window. The seats in front of them were empty.

With a lurch and a clatter the train got under way. Stark watched the prairie roll by as they left Guthrie behind them. They were headed southeast on a narrow-gauge track that penetrated deep into the Indian lands. Stark touched the butt of his Colt. Holdups weren't unknown in this region. The Daltons were still at large despite the best efforts of Heck Thomas and other such stalwart lawmen to corral them.

"I sent a telegram to let Clete know we were coming," Brian said. He caught Stark's frown. "What's wrong?"

"Maybe nothing, but once somebody in Doaksville knows our plans, it stands to reason the Widow Danner can learn them too. The less other folks know about our business, the better off we are for now."

"I should've thought of that," Brian admitted with a hangdog expression. "Won't happen again."

Stark turned his glance back out the window. The chances of a holdup had just gotten a little better, he calculated.

But they pulled into South McAlister late that afternoon without incident. Stark motioned the kids to stay in their seats while the other passengers filed out. Through the window, Stark studied the ramshackle depot. Only a handful of people were milling about there. Some horses were tied at a hitching rail, among them a magnificent golden palomino, he noted with a horseman's eye.

"Let's go." He pushed up from his seat and hefted the war bag down from the overhead rack. He shifted it to his left hand, leaving his right free. The bag was awkward in the narrow lane between the seats. He led the way to the exit.

On the platform he paused, blocking the pair behind him. The cool autumn air felt good after the stuffiness of the passenger car. Once more he ran his eyes over the station.

Maybe he'd been wrong thinking there'd be some sort of hostile welcoming committee awaiting them.

Then he went taut. Maybe he hadn't been wrong after all.

He wasn't sure how he'd missed him in the first place. Leaning with casual insolence against the wall of the depot next to a vacant bench, wrists crossed low across his belly, was a figure that Stark recognized with some startlement as that of an Argentine gaucho, one of the nomadic cowboys of the South American pampas.

There was no mistaking the *chiripá* girding his lean waist, the colorful woolen poncho draping his broad shoulders, or the pleated trousers—the *bombachas*—gathered at the ankles over polished leather boots. Only the wide-brimmed Mexican sombrero was out of keeping with the traditional garb. The hat was tilted forward far enough to hide the features of its owner's face, but not far enough, Stark guessed, to keep him from peering from beneath it at all that went on around him.

Frozen, Stark squinted. The gaucho's folded arms raised the edge of the poncho enough for him to see the fancy tooled gunbelt hung with a holstered revolver and some sort of bowie-style knife in a sheath. And coiled on his other hip was the tapering black thickness of a rawhide—a bull-whip—favored tool and weapon of that robust breed.

Stark knew another fighting man when he saw one. The lazy, slouched stance was all smoke and mirrors; he'd used it sometimes himself to throw enemies off guard. With wrists crossed that low, gun or knife or whip could be brought into play with a flick of the arm. He never for a moment doubted the gaucho's ability to handle the weapons, nor that his own shrewd appraisal was being returned with interest.

At his back, Brian muttered something disparaging, and Stark caught the sharp hiss of Brenda's indrawn breath.

"Who is he?" Stark demanded tersely without looking around.

"That's Juan," Brian answered bitterly. "He's the widow woman's *segundo*. His brother, Jorge, works for her also."

"There's two of them?" Stark's eyes flicked about, but the segundo appeared to be alone.

He was a scout, then, checking out the opposition, Stark decided. He had been right in his hunch; the Widow Danner had known they were coming. Well, maybe he could just give the gaucho something else to report to his patron. He made to step down off the platform, his gaze intent on the segundo.

Abruptly Juan pushed away from the wall. Stark had a moment's view of the sardonic, hawklike face of a ravisher and a despoiler, split by a black mustache that curved up like Old Nick's horns. With swift, flowing steps the gaucho crossed to the magnificent palomino stallion at the hitchrail.

He caught the cantle of the tooled black saddle with both hands, and swung himself astride. Only then did his boots slip neatly into the stirrups as if they belonged there. In a single instant he seemed to become a part of the animal he rode.

A touch of the reins was enough to wheel the palomino away. Stark got the impression of some sort of foreign gear, not common to a western saddle, attached to the fancy hull.

Juan took the palomino off at a casual gallop, as easy and smooth as his own stride had been. He wasn't running, Stark knew. There would be no fear of conflict or confrontation in this one. He was doing a job, obeying orders. When the time came to fight, Juan would be ready.

Stark watched him go with hooded eyes. If her segundo was a sample of her home crew, Norene Danner looked to be a worthy foe even for the Peacemaker.

Chapter Four

" "There's Clete!" Brian exclaimed. "I figured he'd be here."

Stark followed his pointing finger and saw a grizzled oldster handling the lines for the four mules pulling a heavy freight wagon.

Brenda hurried down the steps from the platform and raced the short distance to the wagon. The ancient teamster pulled it to a halt barely in time for her to clamber up to the seat and give him an enthusiastic hug.

"Come on." Brian jerked his head for Stark to follow. "I'll introduce you." He followed more slowly in his sister's wake.

Stark held back, casting his gaze down the road where the gaucho had vanished, then taking a look at what he could see of the town. The train's arrival had sparked some activity. Folks were disembarking to be greeted by towns-people, or to head back along the platform to collect their baggage. A ways down the wide main street Stark spotted the courthouse where'd he need to file Prudence's petition.

He looked about as the driver brought the wagon close up beside the platform, handling it with the careless ease of long practice. The massive vehicle was one of the dependable conveyances manufactured by the Irish wheelwright, Joseph Murphy, which, along with the Conestogas and Studebakers, had served as mainstays of the freight industry in its tumultuous heyday. Stark classed it as one of the big three-ton models.

The original red and blue paint was long since gone, but a fairly recent coat spoke well of the care that had been taken of the vehicle. Stark had heard no grinding of metal on metal, meaning the wheels and axles had been kept greased as well.

Brenda was perched in the seat beside the mule skinner, while Brian had scrambled into the empty bed. The hickory bows, which could be arched over the bed and covered with canvas, had been removed. Likely that was for ease in loading and unloading freight. A tarp tied over a load could serve just about as well in protecting it from the elements if the need arose.

"Jim Stark, this here's Clete Hatfield." Brian stood erect in the bed as he made the introduction. "He's our foreman; he worked with Pa from the very beginning of the B&B."

Stark eyed Clete, who wasn't any too bashful about returning the favor. Like Stark, he didn't seem inclined to speak. The B&B foreman was small and wiry, and looked to be all stringy muscle stretched over bone. His leathery face was aged by long decades of rough living and constant exposure to the weather. He wore faded denims and an equally faded blue shirt. A battered trail hat with the front brim pushed up almost flat against his forehead was settled firmly down on his ears.

The coiled form of a rawhide bullwhip rested by his feet.

At his waist, Stark could make out a massive old revolver of some sort. Shells bigger than those for Stark's .45 filled the loops of an unadorned gunbelt.

"Howdy," Stark broke the silence at last with a laconic greeting. Brian and Brenda were watching the two of them closely.

Clete gave a curt nod of acknowledgment. Stark couldn't tell if he was much impressed with what he'd seen.

The old mule skinner spoke over his shoulder to Brian in a voice as rough as his weathered features. "Best be getting your gear from this iron horse. I got a load of goods to pick up from Suttles Store before we head back."

"I'll hitch up with you there," Stark spoke up. "I've got some papers to file over to the courthouse. Be obliged if you'd collect my trunk and my sorrel."

"Sure thing," Brian told him.

Clete gave the lines a negligent flip, and the two teams of mules thrust obediently against the traces to start the wagon moving. Clete hadn't bothered to set the brake for the brief halt. Seemed he and his teams had come to an understanding, Stark mused wryly. Like the wagon, the animals appeared to be in good shape.

A few townsfolk and passengers moved aside as Clete eased the heavy wagon on toward the freight cars. Brenda flung a quick excited smile back at Stark. Trouble and all, she was still plainly pleased to be home.

Stark hoofed it to the courthouse. He had little difficulty filing Jacob Langton's will and the petition Prudence had prepared to accompany it. Idly he speculated on how she would've ranked his brief performance in the legal field. He recalled the way she'd looked in the calico dress that morning, then resolutely put his mind on other matters.

Following the directions the court clerk had provided, he reached Suttles General Store as the Langtons and their foreman, along with the storekeeper, were finishing up loading the Murphy wagon. Their cargo seemed to consist of a little bit of everything, from foodstuffs, to clothing, to tools, to a brand-new rocking chair that was carefully tied atop the rest of the cargo. The survival of a line like the B&B, Stark knew, depended on its willingness to transport every sort of good or product a farmer, rancher, or settler might want.

It was getting late in the day when they headed out to the southwest across the prairie. His war bag stowed in the wagon, Stark straddled Red with both his shotgun and the long-range sporting rifle sheathed on the saddle. Brian forked the remaining Langton horse, while Brenda kept her place beside the gruff Clete on the seat of the lumbering wagon.

"Reckon we can cover some miles before we pitch camp," the old mule skinner commented as they left town.

"Clete, how's Josh?" Brenda asked with a note of hesitancy. She twisted about some on the seat to eye him anxiously.

Clete snorted. "Durn fool was all het up to be the one to come meet the two of you. I told him not to get uppity with me, and to stay and hold the fort."

Brenda smiled with evident relief. "Then he's all right? And he wanted to come meet me—I mean, us—in South McAlister?"

"Just said that, didn't I?"

Brenda settled more comfortably on the rocking seat and began to hum happily to herself.

The creases on Clete's face deepened in a scowl. He looked about at Stark riding alongside with his small arsenal of firearms. "You look like you're fixing to fight a war," he opined sourly.

"If I do fight one, I don't plan on losing it."

"Listen to the man," Clete jeered.

Stark glanced around at him. "The question I got for

you old-timer,'' he drawled, ''is whether you can really shoot that cannon you're packing without busting your wrist.''

Clete snorted again, shifted the lines in his right hand to his left, and hauled the monstrous hog leg clear of leather with evident pride. ''I can manage a shot or two without it crippling me,'' he said in a challenging tone. ''Ever seen anything like it?''

Stark took his time about answering. He studied the pistol and the knobby hand that gripped it. Clete had the thick wrist of a man who'd spent a lifetime working the heavy ribbons of the big wagons, and wielding a rawhide to control the cantankerous teams of mules and oxen that pulled them. Probably he could shoot the gun, at that.

''Beaumont-Adams revolver,'' Stark identified the weapon aloud. ''Five shot, .54 caliber, British military.'' With the stopping power of an old Sharps buffalo gun, or his own sporting rifle, the Beaumont-Adams was a formidable piece of firepower for a man who could handle it. ''Mighty mean weapon,'' he added.

Clete actually reared back a little bit with surprise. ''Here's a man that knows his guns, just like they say,'' he acknowledged, and slid the revolver once more into his holster. ''Yeah, I done heard of you before now, Mr. Peacemaker. Word is, you was riding shotgun with Zeke Smith when the Ollin boys tried to take the mine payroll up north. The two of you dropped all four of them, with nary a scratch to show for it. Is that true?''

''True enough.''

Clete gave a shake of his grizzled head. ''Well, then you fellows were all-fired lucky!''

''Grace of God,'' Stark corrected.

''Now, by heavens, you remind me of Mr. Alexander Majors himself!'' Clete exclaimed. ''He was a God-fearing man for sure. Before any of us in the Express hit the trail for the first time to make our runs, he gave us a Bible. I still carry mine with me to this day when I'm on the trail.'' He delved under the wagon seat and came up with a battered volume wrapped in oilcloth. "Never would've made it all these years without the Good Book to see me through."

Stark was staring at him. "You rode with the Pony Express?"

Clete gave an emphatic nod and brandished the Bible. "For a fact. Signed up at the very beginning. A pistol, a knife, a stripped-down saddle and mailbags, and a good grain-fed horse was all we had to cover a hundred miles in ten hours. We'd carry the mail from Missouri to California and back again in twenty days. Didn't let nothing stop us— not blizzards, or Indians, or the hottest deserts you ever seen."

Stark was honestly impressed. The heroes who had ridden for the Pony Express back in the days before the War Between the States, were the stuff of legend. Stalwarts such as Johnny Fry, David Jay, and Charley Cliff were numbered among them. Buffalo Bill Cody himself had been a part of their ranks.

Conceived by William Russell, of the mammoth freighting line of Russell, Majors and Waddell, the Express had never been a moneymaking concern, but it had done much to open up the country and connect the two coasts.

Clete's build would've made him ideal for the role of a Pony Express rider. Youth, small stature, riding prowess, grit, and fighting ability were the requirements for carrying the mail for the Express.

"A Pony Express rider and a God-fearing man to boot," Stark spoke with sincerity. "I'm honored to be riding with you."

The old teamster spat out of the side of his mouth.

"Likewise, I reckon," he acknowledged gruffly, then bent quickly to stow the Bible back under the seat.

"I'll scout up ahead," Stark offered.

He put heels to Red and took him to a lope. They were well clear of South McAlister, crossing open prairie under the late afternoon sun. Stark's elongated shadow flowed across the grassland beside him. Two scrappy kids and an old Pony Express rider to side him, he reflected. They'd do to ride this trail with, wherever it was leading.

The sun had painted the western horizon with an artist's sweep of blue and violet and pink when Clete called a halt in a hollow sheltered by low grassy buttes. Other than a couple of distant cowpokes and a farming family headed into town, they'd seen no other folks. The Widow Danner's gaucho had vanished into the vastness of the prairie, but Stark couldn't shake the notion that Juan might not be too far away even now.

Brenda proved herself a good cook, turning ham, beans, and corn dodgers into a satisfying repast that found Stark taking seconds. Night had surrounded the camp by the time they'd finished having coffee to wash down the meal.

"Figure we ought to be setting a watch," Clete opined as he tossed the dregs of his coffee out with a flick of his wrist. He hesitated, as though it took an effort to get the next words out. "You got any objections, Peacemaker?"

"About to suggest it myself."

Clete nodded like he'd been paid his due. "Brenda, you take first turn; Brian, you second. Stark here can be third up. I'll handle the last shift."

Stark wasn't used to letting anyone else call the shots in planning strategy or defense, but Clete seemed a capable enough hand at it—not much of a surprise in light of his background. Stark mused over what routes he'd traveled to bring him here.

He slept lightly, rolled up in his blanket against the fall

chill, shotgun at his side. He roused briefly when Brenda awakened her brother to take his turn, and sat up as the youth approached him a couple of hours later.

"Everything's quiet," Brian reported in a whisper.

The fire had burned low. Stark made no effort to replenish it. The flicker of a flame could be seen for a long way on the prairie at night. Toting his shotgun, he mounted almost to the crest of one of the low buttes, and stood for a time gazing out into the sea of darkness. There was no moon. Low clouds slipped like restless spirits across the icy glare of the stars.

Quiet movement in the camp below made him glance behind him. The trim figure of Brenda Langton was rising from her bedding. Placing her feet carefully in the tall grass, she came up toward him. She halted uncertainly a yard or so away. Stark couldn't make out the expression on her face. She was no more than a girlish form in the cloaking darkness. Even the blond of her hair was all but lost in the gloom.

"Better be getting some sleep," he suggested, wondering what had brought her to his side.

She hugged herself tightly. "I know. I was really tired at first, but then I woke up and couldn't get back to sleep."

Stark didn't want to let himself be distracted from his sentry duty, but something was troubling her. "What's the problem?" he queried.

"It's Josh Watkins," she said breathlessly. "I'm worried about him staying at the B&B alone."

The fourth member of the crew, Stark recalled. "You're sweet on him, aren't you?" he said flatly.

She gasped in surprise at his bluntness. "What? Why, no! I mean—" She broke off as she caught the faint gleam of his grin, then ducked her head contritely. "I suppose I deserved that for being so nosy about you and Prudence—

Miss McKay. But, yes, I guess I really am sweet on him. That's why I'm so fretful about him staying all alone.''

"I reckon he'll be safe enough until we get there to-morrow," Stark reassured her. "I don't think Clete would've left him alone if he'd thought there was too much danger. This Widow Danner might've been willing to send hard cases halfway across the territory to bushwhack you and your brother, but if she was going to hit you on your own doorstep, she'd have tried it before now.

"Besides, your Josh isn't part of the family as yet. Things might change down the line, but right now there's no big percentage in doing harm to him. I ain't met the widow, but she seems like a woman who plays her cards mighty careful. Since her hired guns didn't get their chore done, it's my guess she'll wait a spell to see how things stand before she tries anything like that again."

He heard Brenda let out her breath in a soft sigh. "I hope you're right. I've been praying really hard."

"Keep doing that. But now go ahead and get some sleep. You'll need it."

"Thank you." He felt the brief touch of her hand on his arm, then she turned and left him.

Stark hoped his analysis of things had been right.

He shifted positions, prowling the outskirts of the camp a bit. The night breeze was cool, carrying the scents of dust and buffalo grass and sage. It seemed to carry something else, Stark fancied, something that tended to raise the hackles on the back of his neck. But maybe that was only his imagination and the memory of the feline movements of a man swinging astride a big golden palomino stallion. Just what sort of woman would a man like Juan be willing to work for?

Once more he became aware of movement in the camp. This time it was the wiry form of Clete Hatfield that emerged from the darkness at his side. The old man moved like a wraith.

"Everything quiet?" Clete's voice was a murmur.

"Appears to be," Stark temporized.

Clete hawked and cleared his throat. "Heard what you said to the girl," he spoke gruffly.

Stark wondered how the oldster's ears could've caught their whispered talk.

"You had it figured right," Clete went on. "I didn't reckon the boy was in too much danger, or I wouldn't have left him on his lonesome, especially with Brenda mooning away over him like she is. I forted the B&B up pretty good when I saw what was liable to come down the pike after Jacob died. I told Josh to just sit tight and wait for us."

Stark grunted acknowledgment. Clete hadn't come up here to tell him that.

"I got to say I'm obliged to you for looking out for the kids," Clete continued after a moment. "They told me what all you done. Their pa was the best pard I ever had. His young 'un's mean pretty near the world to me. Never had no family to speak of. Got myself hitched once, but she died trying to give me a child. Would've been a son. After that, I decided I'd just stick to mule skinning. Didn't figure I was cut out to be a family man."

Stark guessed Clete wasn't given to sharing much of himself, even with friends. That meant he was a lot like Stark himself. The darkness made this type of talk easier.

"They're good kids," Stark allowed. "Lucky to have you looking out for them."

"Was starting to fret over the way the widow woman was sniffing at the door with her pack right at her heels. Glad to have you riding shotgun with me."

Stark opened his mouth to try to find an answer. Then he went taut at the same instant Clete sucked in his breath sharply.

"You heard it?" the mule skinner demanded in a harsh whisper. "Somebody's out there!"

Stark didn't know if he'd heard it, or seen it, or picked it up in some other fashion. Maybe the breeze had carried an alien scent cleanly to him at last. But Clete was right. Somebody or something was skulking about out there on the prairie beneath the scudding clouds.

"Cover the other side of the camp!" Stark hissed tersely. He had no qualms about taking charge now.

Not waiting to see if he was obeyed, he slipped over the crest of the butte and ghosted down the far side. At its base he paused, shotgun held ready. His eyes were next to useless in the gloom. He listened, sniffed at the air, strained to sense some awareness of whoever or whatever was nearby.

There was only the sigh of the breeze, the scents of the grassland. Restlessly he scouted outwards for a range of a hundred yards, then worked his way around the camp in a circle. Once he imagined he felt the vibrations of fading hoofbeats, but, again, that might've been only his fancy.

At last, defeated, he headed back toward the camp. Somehow realizing he'd been detected, the interloper had faded away like the night breeze.

Clete met him on the butte. "Nothing?" he queried.

"Nothing," Stark confirmed bleakly.

Chapter Five

Back in the early part of the century, the Doak brothers had established a trading post in the cottonwood jungle near the mouth of the Kiamichi River. From those humble beginnings the town of Doaksville had grown to thrive as the bustling capital of the Choctaw Nation in the period prior to the War Between the States. It was there that Brigadier General Stand Watie, the last Confederate general to surrender, had officially ended the war by laying down his arms.

Since those days, the town had sunk into decline. Frame buildings, some of them on their last legs, lined a rutted dirt road that could've used a going-over by a horse-drawn grader. A barber carried on his trade in a tent adjacent to the blacksmith shop. The fanciest establishments in town, Stark noted without surprise, were the saloon, the bank and the store owned by Norene Danner. They were the only ones that bothered with false fronts.

The underbrush and trees were crowding in close behind

40

many of the other sagging structures, already reclaiming the abandoned outer fringes of the town. If everybody pulled up stakes, in another hundred years there'd be nothing left to mark the town's existence but a few crumbling foundations in a tangle of woods and brush.

Townsfolk paused in their comings and goings to eye the returning wagon and its accompanying riders. Several called out friendly greetings to the Langtons. The kids were well thought of hereabouts, Stark noted with approval. The widow didn't have everybody under her thumb.

Ahead was the ornate front of the saloon. A tall wide billboard above the entry bore the name Crimson Lady Saloon in flowing script followed by a surprisingly well done painting of a gorgeous redheaded woman glancing provocatively back over one bare shoulder. The bright red of the lettering matched the hair of the woman's image.

Stark saw a gun-slung hard case duck into the bar at their approach. He also saw a golden palomino stud, fancy hull still in place, tethered among the handful of lesser horses at the hitching rail.

He had just looked back at the door of the saloon when it opened and a woman and two men emerged. He realized at a glance that he was seeing the model for the portrait on the billboard. Good as it was, the painting hadn't done her justice.

"Speak of the devil's daughter," Clete growled. "There's the Widow Danner herself to greet us."

Stark found himself staring. He wasn't sure what he'd expected in Norene Danner—certainly a woman past middle age—but this stunning vision wasn't it. True, she was long past girlhood, but what must've once been striking good looks had blossomed into fulfillment as a heady brand of beauty.

She wore a red dress that was tight enough to leave no doubt of her statuesque womanhood. It didn't show much flesh, but it sure couldn't be thought of as modest. Red hair was piled high above ivory features that might've graced an exotic ancient medallion from some foreign land.

She came languidly to the edge of the elevated board-walk fronting the bar. The movements of her long legs were seductively clear beneath the scarlet fabric of her dress. *Crimson Lady, indeed,* Stark thought.

She halted in the pose of a showgirl on the stage. Her bold gaze rested on the wagon and the riders as they drew abreast.

The two men bulked close behind her. Stark wasn't surprised to recognize the leonine Juan as the taller of the pair. His brother, Jorge, was a shorter, broader version of the segundo, with the traditional narrow-brimmed and low-crowned hat of the gaucho.

Juan stepped forward with a swagger to stand at the side of his boss. His hands were on his hips, near his pistol and bullwhip. Her head topped his shoulder by a couple of inches. Jorge flanked his brother. Late-afternoon sunlight glinted off steel caps on the toes of his fine tooled boots.

"Keep rolling," Stark ordered Clete, then peeled Red away from beside the wagon.

He heard the aged mule skinner's exasperated exhalation of breath, but the wagon kept moving. Stark reined the sorrel up in front of the boardwalk. He used the pressure of his heels to make the stallion dance just a little.

Both gauchos had tensed up. Norene Danner's full lips quirked with what could've been amusement. "Welcome to Doaksville," she greeted in throaty tones.

"Thank you, ma'am." Stark stilled the sorrel.

"I'm Norene Danner. I never did like to be called ma'am. I'm Norene to my friends."

Stark noticed Juan's gaze cut sharply toward her at that. She ignored him. Her own eyes were near the same hue as the gleaming jade drop she wore against the pale skin of her throat.

"Name's James Stark."

"I know. I heard you were coming."

"Good news travels fast." Stark tried to keep part of his attention on the gauchos. It wasn't easy.

"They call you the Peacemaker," she rolled the sobriquet lazily off her tongue. "Is that what you do? Make peace?"

"Usually only after I make war."

Her plucked eyebrows arched. "Maybe that won't be necessary." She looked him up and down. Stark felt like he was a prize stud being judged for a blue ribbon. Then her eyes left him, and he questioned silently how he'd fared.

"But I'm being terribly remiss in my manners, James," she went on. "This is my foreman, Juan." Her hand brushed his shoulder in what was almost a caress.

"We've met," Stark said. "Leastways, after a fashion."

Juan's smile was sardonic. "You move good in the night, *señor,*" he praised with a rippling accent.

"Not good enough, it seems."

Up close, the decadence and violence he'd glimpsed before in the gaucho's face were even more evident. No doubt a dandy with the *señoritas* in his youth, Juan was long past that stage. Only a very foolish or naive girl would be beguiled by the lechery and cruelty lurking in his hawklike features. Either that, or a woman who liked her men hard and ruthless. Stark wondered how many blue ribbons Juan had won.

"You're a long way from home, hombre," he said aloud.

Juan's face clouded. "*Si,* a long way. But there is nothing left in my homeland now for the old breed such as myself and my brother. The pampas has all been fenced by the owners of the *estancias,* the big ranches. They want us only to nursemaid tame cattle. It is not true work for a gaucho. We are men of the open plains. We make our way by *pistola*, and blade, and whip. We are kin to the wild bulls we once ran!''

Passion rode his tones, and for a fleeting moment Stark felt a yearning kinship with him. ''You came to the wrong country, *amigo*,'' he said softly. ''The same thing is happening here.''

Juan's teeth flashed like a puma's grin. ''Ah, but not in these Indian lands. Here a man can take what he wants, as long as he is strong enough to hold it and make it his!''

The feeling of kinship vanished from Stark. ''Depends on who he wants to take it away from,'' he said levelly.

''Such has always been the way for true men.'' Juan jerked his head sidewise. ''Here is my *hermano*, Jorge. He is a man of the old breed—the wild breed—like myself.''

Jorge shifted his feet in an odd movement that made Stark's eyes narrow. Those steel-toed boots could do a powerful lot of damage in a rough-and-tumble, provided their wearer knew how to use them.

Jorge's eyes were as hard and lifeless as that steel on his boots. He had nowhere near the keen wits of his brother. ''I think you make mistake riding for those *niños* and the old one,'' he said in ugly English.

''Way I read things, your boss lady here doesn't have you on the payroll to do any thinking.'' Stark sketched a quick salute with his forefinger to Norene Danner. ''Ma'am.''

As he put Red down Doaksville's rutted main street in the wake of the wagon, he had an instant's impression of the slow dawning of rage in Jorge's dull eyes, and of the angry sardonic twist of Juan's sensual lips.

''Don't be a stranger, Peacemaker!'' Norene's mocking voice floated after him.

He didn't look back.

"Why did you stop to talk to that awful woman?" Brenda exclaimed from her perch beside Clete when Stark drew level with them.

"Just saying howdy to the neighbors."

"You sure believe in taking the bull by the horns," Clete cut off any further recriminations from Brenda.

"She didn't look like any bull I've ever seen," Stark told him.

Clete turned abruptly serious. "Don't let her get on your blind side, son," he warned.

"I don't have a blind side." But Stark remembered the green eyes and the pale skin and the red dress, and he wondered.

"Here's the B&B!" Brian called.

They were just pulling up in front of a modest collection of wood frame structures on the edge of town. Stark tallied a small house, an office fronting a warehouse, and a barn, beyond which he could see a corral.

The wagon hadn't even halted before a thin male figure appeared warily in the doorway to the office, a rifle gripped competently in his hands. The next moment he gave a glad shout, set the rifle hurriedly aside, and dashed out to greet the arrivals.

Brenda was down off the wagon in a flash and rushing to meet him, her annoyance at Stark's actions apparently forgotten. There was a flurried embrace, a rush of words, and, Stark thought, a quick kiss. Then big brother Brian reined his horse up so close that the reunited couple had to draw apart and step back.

"Quit all that tomfoolery!" he ordered. "You're out in public! That's no decent way to behave. Besides, we got work to do. Any trouble while we were gone?" The last question was snapped at the youth.

The latter—Stark reckoned he had to be Josh Watkins,

the subject of Brenda's late-night fretting—didn't seem to be too put off by Brian's hoorawing.

"Everything's fine," he announced, squaring his wiry shoulders. "Other than tending to the stock, I sat tight like Clete told me. A couple of the widow woman's hard cases came sniffing around this morning. I kept them covered from a gunport, and sent them packing. I think they were just trying to throw a scare into me. Didn't work." He grinned with satisfaction.

Stark put him at Brenda's age. He looked to be growing into tall lean manhood, although he didn't have near his full height or strength as yet. Nor had his bony features beneath his crumpled hat achieved their full maturity. Brenda sure didn't seem to find much wrong with him, however. She beamed proudly at him as he made his report, quailing only a little at his mention of the hard cases.

Clete disembarked from the wagon with an agility surprising for his age. Watching him, Stark saw that the spryness cost him an effort.

"See to the wagon, Josh," Brian ordered authoritatively. Contrary to his earlier attitude, he didn't object when Brenda accompanied Josh to carry out his chore.

"Come on," Brian invited Stark, "I'll show you around."

The warehouse, Stark found, contained a bunkroom for the hired hands. Josh and Clete bedded there while the Langton kids occupied the house. All of them took meals in the house. A large lean-to shed had been added to the exterior of the warehouse to shelter the wagons when not in use. The corral behind the barn held a stock shed for the mules, horses, and milk cow. Beyond the corral a couple of acres had been cleared and fenced to provide pasture. A blacksmith shop and tack room were located off the barn. Jacob Langton had planned and built to last, Stark judged.

When Brian went to join the others in unloading the wagon, Stark lingered to prowl a little on his own. Clete had been speaking the truth when he said he'd forted the holdings up in preparation for trouble. Its location in town and the cleared area in the rear already made the B&B a poor target for any sort of raid or assault. Hinged boards, complete with narrow gunports, had recently been added to the windows of the house and office. A couple of good hands with rifles, placed at strategic posts, would be able to give a good account of themselves against a much larger attacking force.

Fire or dynamite was always a danger, but Stark calculated that Norene Danner would only use those tactics as a last resort. She wouldn't be too eager to destroy the very property she was seeking to obtain, particularly right in front of the rest of the town. Besides, fire, once started, didn't care what it burned. The whole town might be put at risk if the B&B went up in flames.

Satisfied, Stark returned to where the B&B crew was just finishing shifting most of the cargo into the warehouse. Some items had been left in the wagon, likely for quick delivery to local customers.

"You timed things about right," Clete drawled wryly. "Here, at least you can lend a hand with this." He flipped a corner of a tarp to Stark who caught it deftly. Together they got it secured over the remaining cargo. The two boys were unhitching the team. Brenda had gone into the house to start supper.

"No point in unloading this," Clete confirmed Stark's guess. "We'll be heading out tomorrow to deliver it hereabouts. You finish looking the place over?"

Stark nodded. "Nice layout. And you got it forted up right good.

Clete grunted at the compliment. "The kids' pa and I built most of this. The barn was already here. Original house that went with it got took by a twister. Left everything else in town standing, so they say. The kids helped us in putting up the rest of the buildings, but they was just knee-high to the mules back then.''

''What's the story on Josh?''

''Jacob took him in a couple of years back. His folks had died of the lung fever. Same thing as got Brian and Brenda's ma. Jacob felt sorry for Josh and offered him room and board for work as a hired hand. He's a good kid, I reckon. Not too surprising him and Brenda would start sparking like they done. Probably no need to, but Brian and me been keeping an eye on them to make sure they don't get out of line. They're already wanting to get hitched, but we laid down the law and said Brenda needed at least another year before she's marrying age. Same for Josh, as far as that goes.''

Stark nodded soberly. ''A man's a fool to rush into anything like that.'' A fleeting image of Prudence McKay flicked irritatingly across his mind.

''Any suggestions on defending the place?'' Thankfully Clete got back to more practical matters.

''A couple of watchdogs sniffing around wouldn't be a bad idea. And a can of coal oil buried at each corner of the premises, where a rifle shot could set it off, would give us some light if they did mount an attack after dark. Might shake them up a little too.''

Clete chuckled. ''I expect it would. I'll see to that myself. And I'll send one of the boys out to the O'Mier place. They got more dogs than they can rightly use. Should be willing to let us have a couple for next to nothing. I figured we'd be pulling lookout duty from here on out, as well.''

''Yep,'' Stark confirmed. ''And everybody goes armed.''

Clete nodded. ''Their pa and me taught the kids how to handle guns.''

Stark recalled Brian and Brenda capably defending themselves against the bushwhackers, and Josh's ready appearance with the rifle when they'd reached the B&B. "So I've noticed."

There was a chance, he supposed, that he was over-reacting to the predatory gleam in the eyes of Norene Danner and her segundo, and what could've been no more than a bungled robbery by road agents. But his gut told him different, and it was better to take some maybe needless precautions than to end up with your gun holstered when the other fellow had already hauled iron.

"What's next on the slate?" Clete was regarding him with a speculative eye.

Stark had already chewed that over. "Come morning, I want to visit the local law, and have a chat with the saw-bones that examined Jacob Langton's body."

"Is that a fact? Well, in that case, reckon I'll mosey along to introduce you."

Chapter Six

Clete sucked in cold morning air through his nose, filling his scrawny chest. "We'll get an early dose of winter this year," he opined. The rawboned mule he straddled flicked its long ears at the sound of his voice, but continued its plodding walk.

Riding at his side, Stark cut a glance at him. "You figure it'll delay making your deliveries?"

Clete shrugged. "Could be. Snow, floods, dust, heat, I've hauled freight through them all. Reckon snow's about the worst."

Stark eyed him curiously. "You ever haul on the Bozeman Trail?" he speculated aloud.

Clete's head dipped in an affirmative nod. "Yep. And the Santa Fe, the Overland, and a few others that ain't even remembered these days. Nothing left of them now but ruts on the prairie. Likely some of those ruts will still be there a hundred years from now." He ruminated for a moment, slouched in his saddle. "After the Express folded, and the

50

War between the States heated up, I signed on with the Union. Was a bullwhacker most of the war, walking beside them oxen, taking them wagons through purgatory and cannon fire to see the boys got their supplies. The Union never would've won if we hadn't kept the wagons rolling.''

"And after the war?'' Stark prodded with genuine interest.

Clete seemed to muse a moment over whether to answer.

"Signed on with Russells, Waddell and Majors again,'' he spoke at last. "Since I'd been an Express rider for them, they hired me as a driver. Later I made wagonmaster. I was always able to find work, even when the big freight companies went under. Did a spell as a stage driver for Butterfield. Finally I teamed up with Jacob Langton.''

Stark gave an admiring shake of his head. The glory days of the old freight lines were gone, but he'd heard the tales of the giant trains, with their hundreds of wagons, stretching off out of sight over the horizon. On the trail, a wagonmaster was like the captain of a ship at sea. His word was law.

"There's the badge-toter's office,'' Clete's scornful tones pulled Stark out of his reverie.

The structure he indicated was little more than a frame shack fronting a tiny brick cell block. Law was scarce here in the Indian lands. Tribal police and the U.S. Marshal's Office shared an uneasy and sometimes overlapping authority. But Guthrie and the U.S. Marshal's Office were a long ways away, and tribal police were few and far between. Communities in the lands could appoint their own peacekeepers, but often the law in Indian Territory was on the side of the fellow with the fastest gun and the quickest trigger.

"What's his handle?'' Stark asked aloud.

"Marshal Horace Bailey. Town council appointed him.

Mostly he rousts drunks, so long as they're too drunk to put up a fight, and don't belong to the Widow Danner.''

"Is she on the council?"

"She's the head of it. Her husband was mayor before he up and fell off his horse. She could've taken his place, but she didn't like the idea of having folks call her 'Mayor.' But she wouldn't hear of anybody else being elected either.''

"You could always run for office," Stark suggested dryly. "You'd have my vote.''

Clete snorted in disgust and swung down from his hull. He moved a little stiffly this morning. "Upshot of it is," he concluded, "she pretty much has the run of things hereabouts.''

Beauty, vanity and power, Stark reflected as he dismounted. That made for a dangerous combination in a female.

Clete wrapped the reins of his mount around the hitching rail. Like a lot of old mule skinners, he favored a mule over a horse. His Beaumont-Adams revolver sagged in its holster on his wiry waist. His coiled bullwhip hung casually on his saddle horn.

Stark touched the butt of his own .45. There was no sign of Norene or her minions around the Crimson Lady. The lifelike picture of the saloon's proprietor still smiled roguishly at him over one bare shoulder.

Clete didn't bother knocking at the lawman's door. He turned the knob and thrust it wide open before entering with a swagger. Stark followed.

The inside of the marshal's office wasn't much of an improvement over the outside. Its occupant fitted his sorry den, Stark thought darkly. Horace Bailey was big, sweaty and balding. His bulk was more suet than muscle, and he stared at his uninvited visitors first with surprise, then anger, showing in his shifty eyes.

He heaved half erect in his overburdened swivel chair. Sweat gleamed on his scalp. It was hot in the office. A stove kicked off enough heat to make the perspiration pop out on Stark's forehead as well. Stark wouldn't have thought a hefty specimen like Bailey would need so much heat to keep warm.

"Hatfield, what the devil do you mean busting into my office thataway?" the marshal blustered. "And who's this big galoot with you?" He appeared to be on the verge of adding a few more comments until he got a good look at Stark.

"This here's the B&B's new hired hand," Clete spoke up quickly. "Monicker of Jim Stark. Lots of folks know him as the Peacemaker." He said the last with wicked relish.

"Heard you'd got yourselves a fancy gunslinger." Bailey was still surly, but he'd lost some of his open hostility. Fumbling on his cluttered desk he came up with a half-filled whiskey bottle. "Snort?" When neither man answered him, he uncorked the bottle, took a swig, and set it back on the desk. He didn't replace the cork. "What can I do for you gents?"

"Answer some questions about the death of Jacob Langton," Stark told him.

Bailey looked genuinely surprised. "He fell off his wagon. What about it?"

"Did you examine the place where it happened?"

"Examine it? Why should I do that? You think I go trotting off to snoop around everytime some cowpoke or farmer breaks an arm or cuts his finger?"

"Langton didn't break his arm or cut his finger. He had his neck broken and his skull crushed," Stark reminded.

Bailey lifted his big shoulders in a shrug. "So he died. Accidental death. Even Doc Harrison said so. Langton was a nice enough fellow, I reckon. A bit stubborn and mule-headed, if you ask me. Course, I won't speak ill of the dead. Maybe he fell asleep, or got drunk, and fell on his head. I don't rightly know how it happened.''

"Jacob wasn't a drinking man," Clete advised bluntly.

Bailey blanched. He took a drink himself. "Well all right. No offense meant of the dead, but I still don't see as how this is any of my concern. My job's to keep the peace here in Doaksville." He brightened at a sudden thought. "Anyways, that accident happened outside of town. That's plumb beyond my jurisdiction." He drew a sigh of relief.

Stark felt his lips thin in disgust. He hadn't expected much else, but that didn't mean he had to like what he was finding. "Thanks for your help," he said laconically. "Don't be surprised if your job of keeping the peace gets a little harder directly."

"I won't stand for any trouble in—" Bailey blustered. The closing of the door behind Stark and Clete cut him off.

"Fine figure of a lawman," Stark commented wryly.

"Ain't he though? Don't figure he'd side with the widow and her gunhands if push came to shove, but he sure wouldn't do nothing to stop her having her way."

"It's the same thing."

"Yeah, I reckon." Clete pointed with his chin. "Down there's the doc's place."

The local sawbones had himself a frame house with an attached office area. A long-dead garden, overgrown by equally dead weeds, was next to the porch. It reminded Stark of a grave. A small barn and corral were visible out back. Probably where the doctor carried on his veterinary practice. The one horse Stark could see looked to be on its last legs.

A bell rang as they entered the waiting area. Harrison himself appeared from the rear of the building. He was tall and sallow, with dyspeptic features below receding color-less hair. His body looked loose and flaccid. Nicotine stained all of his fingers, and a quirley drooped from his lips. The smell of scorched tobacco hung strong in the close air.

"Yes, gentlemen?"

Clete did the honors. Harrison bobbed his head throughout. "I don't know what I can tell you, but come on back," he invited when Clete finished.

His office was dark, and could've used an early spring cleaning. Cigarette smoke drifted in lazy layers. Stark decided he didn't have any wish to see the good doctor's examining room, as a patient or otherwise.

Harrison drew on his quirley and hitched a bony hip onto one corner of his desk. He regarded his visitors owlishly.

"Where was Langton's body when you examined it?" Stark asked.

"Right in there in my examination room." Harrison nodded toward a connecting doorway.

"So you didn't see the site of the accident?" The questions were old hat to Stark, part of the training he'd acquired back East during his days with the Pinkertons.

"There was no need for me to go see where it happened," Harrison answered with a touch of belligerence.

Stark kept his tone level. "Was he dead by the time you examined him?"

"Sure was."

"Did you write up a report?"

"No, I didn't write up any report!" Harrison snapped. "What do you think this is, some big-city hospital? I told the marshal the cause of death and that was the end of it!"

Unexpectedly Harrison's eyes bulged, and he barely had time to snatch the quirley from his lips before he doubled forward in a convulsion of hacking coughs that, Stark thought, bid fair to break his spare form in half like a brittle stick. Gasping, he straightened at last and pulled hard on the cigarette he still held in his yellowed fingers.

"What was the cause of death?" Stark resumed.

Harrison blinked tears from his eyes. The coughing spell had drained some of the anger from him. "I'm not sure," he managed. "Could've been a broken neck; could've been a fractured skull. Either one might've done it."

"Then they were inflicted at approximately the same time."

Harrison nodded weakly. "Simultaneously, so far as I could tell."

"Were they the type of injuries you'd normally expect to result from a fall out of a slow-moving wagon?"

Harrison exhaled smoke through his nostrils and drew in more from his cigarette. He appeared to gain strength from the exchange. "They seemed a little severe for that type of accident," he conceded. "But a fall like that could've caused them both."

Stark let it ride. "Did the accident occur in open country?"

"I can answer that," Clete offered. "Wasn't far from town. There was some underbrush and trees and such alongside the road." He sounded puzzled over Stark's reason for the question.

"Was there anything unusual about the body, aside from the fatal injuries?" Stark asked Harrison.

The doctor's quirley was all but searing his fingers. He dropped it absently, stepped on it and ground it into dust. The floor was thick with a residue of ashes and powdered tobacco. Face pinched in thought, Harrison drew out a bag and papers and began to roll a replacement. The whole routine was so automatic that Stark was sure he could've performed it in the dark.

"There were some minor abrasions that weren't unusual," Harrison answered at last. "But in addition there were some welts on his neck."

"Welts?"

Harrison nodded firmly. "Almost like rope burns."

"You mean from a noose?" Stark demanded.

"No. It was more like he'd been struck by a rope or heavy piece of leather."

"A bullwhip?"

"These weren't wounds from a whip. I'm not sure what caused them, but the skin had been rubbed raw in several overlapping streaks. Since no one knows exactly what happened, I guessed he had sustained them in his fall, maybe from getting tangled up in the reins. But they were unusual."

"Were there any fingerprints?" Stark probed. "Strangle marks?"

Harrison was shaking his head before he finished. "Nope. I've seen all kinds of injuries and wounds from accidents, weapons and bare hands. These welts weren't like none of them."

Far back in Stark's mind, like something in a cocoon, a notion was trying to grow wings and turn into something else. He didn't know what. As yet, it was too soon to tell.

"What about Old Man Danner?" he asked the sawbones.

Harrison stiffened in surprise. "What about him?"

"Heard he died in a riding accident. Any similarities to Jacob Langton?" Stark was conscious of Clete's quick appraising glance in his direction.

Harrison was bemused, but he went ahead and replied. "Now that you mention it, the injuries were similar. That is, the broken neck and the fractured skull."

"What about the abrasions on the neck?" Stark tried to quell the sudden tautness he felt.

Harrison shook his head. "Old Man Danner fell off his horse, got his boot hung in the stirrup, and was dragged a good quarter of a mile. Wasn't much of him that didn't have scratches and abrasions all over."

Blind canyon, Stark thought bleakly. If there were any

definite conclusions to be drawn here, he wasn't able to see them.

"Obliged for your time, Doc," he said tiredly.

"My pleasure," Harrison assured him. "Now, that will be five dollars."

Stark blinked, then paid him wordlessly. He'd put that on the expense account for Prudence to approve, he vowed to himself. Harrison was fumbling to light another quirley as they left.

Outside, Stark drew fresh air into his lungs. "Remind me not to come down sick in this town," he told Clete. "Even if I survived the treatment, I doubt I could afford the cost."

Clete started to answer, then broke off as Stark lifted his head like a wolf catching a scent on the breeze. He turned his own eyes in the direction of Stark's gaze.

The Crimson Lady Saloon was slantwise across the road from them. Four burly yahoos had just descended from the boardwalk in front and started purposefully in their direction.

"Trouble," Stark said needlessly.

"Looks like the widow wants you to make some war."

Chapter Seven

None of the quartet were packing iron, Stark saw quickly. Bruisers. A knuckle and skull dustup then, he mused. Behind the hard cases he saw the striking scarlet figure of Norene Danner appear, flanked by Juan and Jorge. The three of them stayed on the boardwalk, apparently content to watch the fun. Stark thought he detected the same mocking challenge on Norene's ivory features that he had heard in her tone when they'd parted the day before. She wasn't wasting any time putting the spurs to him.

"I'll handle them," Stark said, not taking his eyes off the rowdies. He was cutting a big slice for himself, he knew. Maybe too big.

Clete snorted in answer. "Teach your granddaddy to ride a mule, youngster," he drawled, and went forward ahead of Stark to meet the trouble.

The four bruisers had spread out in a rough half circle. Stark and Clete moved clear of Red and the mule tethered at the hitchrail. A spooked mount was nothing to be close to in a fracas. Flailing hooves could do as much damage as fists and boots.

"You boys got business with us?" Stark said coolly as he came to a halt. A few townsfolk were gathering to see the goings-on.

All four of the toughs were husky specimens. They didn't seem too concerned about not being armed. It figured they were old hands at this. Stark contemplated hauling iron on them, but he didn't hanker to start shooting unarmed men. Besides, he was an old hand at this too.

One of the middle pair gave a gap-toothed grin. "We ain't looking for trouble. We're just headed to see the doc."

"We'll get out of your way," Stark drawled.

Still grinning, the spokesman shook his head. "I don't think so."

Stark shrugged. "Well, then you're headed down a mighty rough trail, pardner."

"We're up to it."

Nothing else needed to be said. The four of them closed in fast. Probably by plan, the hombre on the far left went for Clete. The other three converged on Stark like a prairie twister.

They were quick, and they moved together. Stark didn't have time to get in the first lick. In an instant he was the target of a half dozen battering fists. He moved back just enough to keep any of them from getting behind him. Then he could only raise his fists and forearms up in front of his face like a prizefighter, hunch his shoulders, and let the twister rip into him.

Hard knuckles punished his forearms, pounded his shoulders. One punch got through to rattle his jaw, another set his ears to ringing. He took quick aim and lashed out sidewise with his boot, stamping at a denim-clad knee to his left. The owner of his target howled and staggered, lurching back a step.

Arms still up to guard, Stark shifted weight and drove his leg out at the hombre on his right. This time his booted foot met a solid midriff. As with the knee-kick it didn't put his foe out of the fight, but it gave him time at last to face the man in front of him head-on.

He snapped his left arm to block a freewheeling right that was meant to knock him silly. Wavering not a bit, he drove his own right in a short wicked arc, turning it just a little as he did. His hard knuckles collided with a bony jaw. The brawler was rocked back. Stark thrust his foot straight out, twisting his hips into the movement. The yahoo folded over his boot like a jackknife. The push behind the kick drove him still further backwards. Stark stepped fast after him, swung his stiffened leg up and hammered his boot heel down hard to the back of the offered neck. The fellow went flat on his face across a rut and lay still.

A solid weight cannoned into Stark from behind and sent him stumbling over the fallen man. He'd taken too long in dispatching that one, he realized, and given his pards time to get back into the fray. Concern rose in him at the notion of going down and having these hombres put the boot to him.

He caught himself on his palms and twisted onto his side as the boots started to fly. A pointed toe rammed his spine like a red-hot poker. A heel barely missed his head as he ducked. He swung a leg as if it was a scythe and cut the feet of one attacker cleanly from under him. Rolling onto his back he flicked his feet—one-two—up at the form of the other man looming above. One boot drove into softness, the other struck hard bone. The brawler yelled and reeled aside.

Stark catapulted to his feet. The hombre whose legs he'd swept from under him was also lurching erect, trying to get himself set. Stark never gave him the chance. With his shoulder behind them, he drove short chopping blows to the head and face and dumped the bruiser back onto the street. Rolling over, the fellow started to crawl away.

Stark wheeled toward the other brawler. As he turned he had a glimpse of a disheveled Clete clubbing the barrel of his big Beaumont-Adams pistol down across the head of the fourth hombre. The bigger man sagged. Outmatched by size and age, Clete apparently didn't have any qualms about evening the odds a little.

The uneven pound of booted feet alerted Stark. He side-stepped without looking as the remaining hombre came at him in a hobbling rush, slinging out a long right hand. Stark added a shove, and the force of the fellow's rush carried him past Stark and all the way to the hitching rail. Red and the mule snorted and shied away as far as their ties would allow. Their hooves churned up dust from the street.

The final rowdy was game. He came lurching out of the dust, still spoiling for a fight. Stark gave it to him. He flipped one foot up in a high arc at the man's jaw, swept it in a reverse of the same movement without his boot ever touching down. The bruiser's head snapped back and forth beneath the kicks. He tottered but didn't go down. The widow and her pet wolves had wanted a show, Stark thought with dark satisfaction as he faded back a step to get room. Well, they'd get one.

Dirt sprayed from under his feet as he flung himself into the air, legs tucked beneath him. He went hurtling at his opponent, and his right leg snapped out straight. The sole of his boot, driven by the whole force of the leaping kick, hit the rowdy's chest like a battering ram. The fellow flew past the mounts, hit the hitching rail, and flopped completely over it in a clumsy backwards somersault. He lay still in the dust raised by his landing. A yell of acclaim went up from one of the watching townspeople.

Stark crouched, putting a hand on Clete's saddle to

steady himself. The mule tried to snap at him with square yellow teeth.

"Pistol-whip me, will you?" a man's snarling voice brought Stark sharply around. "I'll carve you open, you old geezer!"

Clete's foe had recovered faster than he'd had any right to. Stark didn't know exactly what had happened, but Clete must've turned to watch him finish the final bruiser, only to be blindsided by the rowdy he'd felled with his pistol. Now the gun lay in the street out of reach, and the hard case had come up with an ugly skinning knife. Hunched like a stalking cat, he closed in on the old man, who faced him determinedly.

Stark's hand shot out. He snatched Clete's bullwhip from where it hung on the pommel of his saddle. The leather-bound handle settled into Stark's palm with an easy familiarity, and the coils fell loose. It had been a spell since he'd wielded a rawhide, but he sensed that the old skills were still there.

He whirled the whip in a blurring circle over his head, straightening his arm to its full length, as he stepped forward to put his whole body into the movement. He didn't use his wrist. He let the weight of the whip itself pop the lash to its full length. The knife was a small target, ten feet distant, weaving a little in its owner's fist. Instinctively Stark aimed low and to the left. He heard the crack of displaced air, but even for him it was impossible to see the leather thongs—the poppers—at the tip of the whip wrap themselves around the knifeman's wrist and wring the weapon from his grip.

The bruiser howled in pain. His knife sailed through the air. Stark jerked the whip clear, again using the circular movement to keep it from popping back into his own face as he recovered it.

Clete spent only an instant gawking before diving for his

gun. The rowdy cursed and went for his fallen knife. Before Stark could strike again another ear-splitting pop rang through the air. The fallen knife skittered from under its owner's reaching fingers.

And Juan, down in the street where he'd leapt from the boardwalk, was retracting his whip with the same overhead arc Stark had used. Beneath his sombrero, his face was alight with a savage grin.

"Enough!" he shouted. "These two have beaten you sorry dogs. Go on! Go away and lick your wounds!"

The thwarted bruiser straightened, rubbing his wrist.

"You heard the man!" Norene Danner had to speak around the crimson fingernail she was withdrawing from between even white teeth. Stark saw she'd bitten it in two. Her ivory features were flushed, her eyes bright, as she stared at the carnage on the street. She'd be the kind who enjoyed watching the cockfights, too, Stark mused.

Two of the brawlers were picking themselves up under the menacing barrel of Clete's pistol. The man Stark had kicked over the hitchrail lay where he had fallen, chest rising and falling slowly. Dust still hung in the air.

Without thinking about it, Stark recoiled the whip. Juan was doing the same. His mouth hadn't lost that challenging grin. Stark's eyes dropped to the lash in the gaucho's calloused hands. Gleaming black, made of braided leather, it was longer than Clete's whip. A good sixteen feet in length, Stark judged. And its end wasn't composed of the thong poppers used to sting the hip of an unruly team animal. Instead, Juan's rawhide ended in a slightly enlarged tip. A pellet of lead had been sewed into the leather.

Fighting man's whip, Stark knew. Not a tool to be used for mule skinning, but a weapon that was meant to be used for man skinning instead.

Stark went toward him. Both hands gripping his coiled

whip low in front of him, Juan cocked his head curiously. As Stark neared him, his chin lifted in acknowledgment.

"You use the rawhide," he commented.

"Done a little mule driving in my day."

"No, I think you have done more than that." Juan's fists tightened on his own whip until his big knuckles stood out whitely. "Me, I use the rawhide too. But I do not drive mules. I drive men."

"Mules don't carry whips. Some men do."

"*Sí,* that is why it is more interesting to drive men."

"More dangerous also,"

Juan's wicked smile widened. "Exactly, *mi amigo.*"

"I'll stick to mules," Stark said mildly.

Juan tilted his head back a little and laughed. His eyes never left Stark's face. "Again, I do not think so. But the rawhide is not the only weapon you use. This fighting with *los pies*—the feet—what do you call it?"

"Savate," Stark told him.

Juan's handsome brow furrowed briefly in thought. "French," he announced then with remembrance. "The fists and the feet."

"That's right."

"Ah, and you have perhaps studied it in France?"

"Some."

Juan glanced briefly back over his shoulder at the stolid form of his brother, Jorge, still on the boardwalk beside the widow. Whatever meaning the look carried, Stark couldn't determine. Jorge gave that peculiar little shuffle of his steel-toed boots.

Stark shifted his gaze past Juan to Norene Danner. She met his eyes boldly. "I think I've got business with your *patrón,*" Stark told the gaucho.

Sudden tension tautened Juan's body, but he stepped aside. Stark edged by him. He didn't like having Juan behind him, but it couldn't be helped. Clete, with his big hand cannon, could cover his back.

Norene glided to the very edge of the elevated board-walk, placed a hand languidly on an upright, and swayed her body against it. She wore another red dress, cut low in front and slit high up on one side. Today the crimson mane of her hair hung loose. Her emerald eyes moved boldly over Stark.

"Enjoy the show?" he inquired laconically. He didn't need to ask. She'd eaten it up like a cat with a bird.

The tip of her tongue salved her scarlet lips. "Now I've seen you make war."

Stark shook his head. "Not yet. This was barely a skirmish."

Her eyes widened mockingly. "So there's more to see?"

"Keep pushing the B&B and you'll find out." Stark's tone was flat.

"I wasn't pushing the B&B," she explained lazily. "I was actually testing you. I wanted to see if you were as tough as Juan seems to think."

"Juan thinks I'm tough?" Stark echoed sardonically.

"Yes, he does."

"And what about you?"

She made a husky purring noise in her throat. He didn't know what it signified. She rubbed against the upright, and the slit in her gown gaped indecently to reveal a pale length of gleaming leg.

Stark was conscious of movement about him. Juan passed him to mount the steps to the boardwalk. He started to resume his place beside Norene, but she shifted away from the upright so that he was forced to stay behind her. Stark glimpsed a brief angry scowl on his face.

Clete edged up even with Stark. His pistol was still held casually in his knobby fist. Stark looked back over his shoulder at the street. Three of the defeated rowdies were beating a shuffling retreat. Two of them had to help the third to walk. They didn't seem very worried about their senseless cohort who hadn't moved from the dust behind the hitching rail. Clete's ornery mule was stretching his long neck against the reins, trying to reach down and nip his prone shape.

"You and I need to talk," Norene's voice drew Stark's attention back to her. "Alone."

Peremptorily she turned toward the door to the saloon. Juan hesitated, then stepped aside, the muscles of his jaw working like he was worrying a chaw of tobacco. Norene paused and glanced back over her shoulder at Stark in an almost exact duplication of her pose on the billboard. "Coming?" she asked archly.

Clete gave a quick admonishing shake of his head. Stark ignored it. He mounted the steps and followed Norene into the Crimson Lady.

Chapter Eight

The barroom was far too elegant for a town like Doaksville. Stark followed the saloon owner's swaying figure past the length of a fine mahogany bar, complete with mirror and racked bottles behind it. She slipped gracefully among the gaming tables without looking back.

Business was light this early in the day. What few patrons there had been had filtered out to see the fight. A thin-faced barkeep polished glasses and observed them without expression. An early rising floozy kept him company, nursing a drink. In the mirror, Stark could see she wasn't as pretty as her boss. He wasn't one for the gaming tables, but he would've been willing to bet that Norene Danner didn't have any woman on her payroll who came close to matching her in looks.

He tailed her down a passage leading off from the barroom, trying not to notice the occasional flash of leg through the slit in her dress. He had a sudden hunch that Daniel might've felt a little like this when he was being led to the lion's den. Difference was, Daniel had been forced to go. He was fool enough to go in by choice. There was something else in Scripture, he recalled, about an ox being led to slaughter.

Still, he told himself, maybe he could learn something about this woman who was the enemy. But was that the only reason he was going? a sly voice pestered him by asking.

"Here." She used a key she had produced from somewhere on her person to open a heavy paneled door.

No lion's den was ever this sumptuous, nor any slaughterhouse, he reflected as he stepped through the doorway.

Plainly these were her private chambers. There was plenty of plush furniture, upholstered in shades of pink and red—a couch, a chaise longue, easy chairs. A thick rug yielded under his boots. Exotic jade figures adorned the carved mantel over the fireplace, and a display of peacock plumes in a tall vase gleamed green and blue and violet in the light from the oil lamps. A roulette wheel and a small bar were tucked into a corner. Another door led off into what he glimpsed was a boudoir. The sweetish scent of some sort of heady incense hung in the close air.

He moved further into the cloying atmosphere, then caught his breath and halted abruptly as he saw the painting dominating one wall. It was a life-size oil of a voluptuous woman half-reclining on a chaise longue such as the one positioned beneath it. Only a few silken strips concealed the figure of the artist's redheaded subject. As with the portrait on the sign for the saloon, that subject was clearly Norene. The artist had captured her nicely with sensual strokes of oil on canvas.

She stopped and turned so sharply that she was almost pressed against him. She had anticipated his reaction to the painting and planned for just this instant to take advantage of it.

"Not many men have seen that, James."

Stark tore his eyes away from the beguiling work and looked down into her upturned face. A heady musk, suddenly stronger than the incense, filled his nostrils.

"What about Juan?" he heard himself ask. "Has he seen it?"

She gave a throaty chuckle and stepped back a bit. "Juan knows his place with me. You and he are a lot alike, you realize."

"Not so much."

She shrugged the subject aside and cocked her head to study the painting with obvious pleasure. "My husband had that done. After we came to this town, he commissioned an artist from back East to travel all the way out here and paint it. He was very proud of it."

"So are you."

She cut her emerald eyes sidewards at him, amusement sparkling in them. "That's right; I am."

"It's a nice work," Stark said dismissively.

She gave another chuckle and turned to cross to the bar. From beneath it she produced a bottle of what Stark thought was good Kentucky bourbon. He doubted her customers out front in the barroom ever got a taste of it.

"Drink?" She lifted the bottle. The lamplight caught the amber fluid.

"I'm not much for drinking."

"Oh?" She arched her eyebrows coquettishly. "Afraid you'll lose your head?"

He was more likely to lose his soul in this place, Stark mused. Lion's den or no, she was certainly as dangerous as a lioness. "Haven't lost it yet," he said aloud.

"Is that so? Well, here's to men of iron." She poured into a shot glass, licked the rim, then swallowed it smoothly with no apparent effect. Woman of iron.

Pouring another, she left the bar and moved languidly to

the chaise longue, clearly aware of his eyes on her. With rehearsed ease she sank down onto it in exactly the same pose as the painting on the wall above. She lapped once at her drink, then leaned to place it on a low ornate coffee table before resuming her pose.

"Come sit down," she invited.

Stark wished he had taken the drink. It would've given him something to do with his hands. The room suddenly seemed even warmer than the marshal's office had been. There was space beside her on the longue, but he strode to a chair nearby and dropped into it. Her eyes mocked him.

"Tell me about the Peacemaker," she requested.

Stark was feeling like he'd been feinted out of position in a *savate* match. "Tell me about the Crimson Lady," he parried.

She preened. It was plainly a subject she liked. What do you want to know?"

"For starters, why do you stay in Doaksville?"

"Because I have something here I wouldn't have any-where else," she answered with sudden passion. "My husband first saw me on the stage at a hurdy-gurdy joint in Chicago. He'd come there from the Territory on business, and when he saw me, he decided to bring me back with him. I told him I'd go, but only as his wife." She smiled with a trace of cruelty. "By then, he didn't put up too much of an argument. Anyway, he brought me here, set me up in luxury, named this saloon after me, and treated me like a queen!"

"And now that he's gone, you're in charge," Stark finished for her.

"That's right!" Wicked satisfaction laced her words. "I own most of what matters in this town, and people work for me. I'm the boss. Do you think I ever would've gotten any of this if I was still flashing my legs on some cheap stage in Chicago?"

She was still flashing her legs, Stark reflected, just on a different stage. He wasn't immune to the sight. "Sounds like your period of mourning is over."

"I did my mourning back on that stage in Chicago, before I ever met him," she declared fiercely. "He got what he wanted from me, and now I've got what I wanted from him!"

"His life?" Stark inquired.

Her eyes blazed. "His death was an accident!"

"Just like Jacob Langton's."

She gave her head an angry toss. Her crimson tresses whipped across her shoulders. "Yes!" she snapped. "Accidents happen, especially to older men who insist on riding spirited horses, or handling heavy freight wagons."

He'd angered her, Stark saw, but there was no vestige of guilt that he could spot. "Why set your sights on the B&B?" he asked. "You've got everything you could want. Why try to put your brand on a two-bit freight outfit?"

Her rage subsided somewhat. "Because I want it! And because Jacob Langton always looked down his nose at me when he was alive. But there's more to it than that. What do you think will happen to this territory, James?"

"Statehood eventually. The government won't let the Indians hang on to these lands forever, no matter what promises were made to them."

"Exactly," she agreed a bit breathlessly. "And when that happens, this area will boom like California did during the days of the gold strikes. All of what I have will be double what it's worth now, even triple! And whoever holds the reins to commerce in this area, whether by freight or rail, will also hold the reins to a lot of other things besides. I want to be that person!"

She leaned invitingly toward him, and suddenly the ambitious businesswoman was replaced by the wanton vamp. "I know you understand that, James. You sell your guns to the highest bidder. You do what you do for money. Isn't that right?''

''I work for whoever hires me.''

She took it as assent. ''I could hire you, James.'' She reached to lay a hand on his knee. He fancied he felt its heated touch even through the denim fabric.

''I don't come cheap,'' he said around a hoarseness in his throat.

''I wouldn't expect you to! I can offer you more than those silly kids, even that pretty little blond schoolgirl. I can give you money and power and more. We can be partners. I need a man beside me, a strong man who can use his brain as well as his fists or his guns. You're that man! We can take this slice of the territory and make it ours, you and me together!''

The moment held its own awful temptation. She rushed on, her fingers tight on his knee. ''All you have to do for the moment is resign from the B&B. The kids and that old man will roll over, and the B&B will be mine.''

''Wouldn't be that easy,'' Stark heard his own voice. ''There's a lady lawyer in Guthrie who'd have something to say about it.''

She flinched as if he'd slapped her. ''What do you mean?'' she demanded, withdrawing her hand.

Stark felt a surge of relief. Remotely he asked himself why he'd brought the subject of Prudence up at all. ''Her name's Prudence McKay. She's the executor of Langton's will, and she's mighty stubborn. Getting rid of me wouldn't solve your problem.''

''What's she to you?'' Norene's query was sharp.

''She hired me as troubleshooter for the freight line.''

''That's all?'' she pressed.

''That's all.''

She studied him as though she could discern things about him he didn't know himself. Her breathing slowed some from its rapid pace. Elements stirred in the facets of her emerald eyes—disappointments, schemes, he couldn't have said. Maybe both. Then her hand moved once more to brush his knee in a lingering caress.

"Remember my offer, James. It will still be open if you change your mind."

Rising abruptly she crossed to the bar and poured herself another drink. As Stark stood to his feet, she lifted it in a kind of salute to him.

"The B&B is off-limits," Stark said flatly.

She might not have heard him. She drank, then lowered her glass. Her lips gleamed with the sheen of the whiskey.

Stark turned away from her knowing grin. He felt drained, as if he'd just won a tougher fight than the one in the street.

"Don't forget what I said, James," her voice caught him at the door.

"Yes, ma'am," he responded without looking around, then left the room. He didn't figure he'd be forgetting her for a good spell to come.

Clete met him in front of the saloon, eyeing him up and down as though looking for scratches. "Wondered if you'd walk out of there in one piece."

"Just barely," Stark said with feeling.

He stepped past the older man and descended to the street. He heard Clete's footsteps behind him.

"Peacemaker!" another voice snarled.

Stark turned sharply. Hands on hips in his familiar pose, Juan towered above them on the boardwalk. Jorge was nowhere in sight. The big gaucho was alone.

Stark felt a sense of shock. Norene Danner must've beguiled him more than he'd realized for him to let Juan come up on him unawares.

"You speaking to me?" he asked mildly.

Juan lifted his head arrogantly. "The woman. She is not for you."

"You're welcome to her if you can hold her, *compadre*," Stark told him.

But the touch of her hand still lingered. He didn't want to be alone with her again. Juan watched them coldly as they mounted.

"Getting old and slow," Clete said ruefully once they'd headed back toward the B&B. "That jasper never should've been able to get the jump on me with that knife."

"My granddaddy never could ride a mule worth a darn," Stark remarked.

Clete's weathered face reddened, then he emitted an explosive guffaw. "Reckon he likely couldn't, at that!" He sobered then. "I'm beholding you."

"Glad to have you siding me," Stark brushed the praise aside.

Clete studied him shrewdly. "You're an old hand with the rawhide. Where'd you learn to handle it like that?"

"I spent a season working for an old mule whacker when I was a youngster. He liked to do tricks with his whip: popping a coin off a fence post, snuffing out a candle, snatching a cigarette from out of a man's mouth. He taught me all those stunts."

"Taught you something more than that, I'd wager. I seen the way you looked at Juan's whip. That's a fighting whip."

"It wasn't meant for a mule," Stark agreed darkly.

"Used to have me one like that myself. Never thought I'd have need of it again." Clete cut another appraising glance at Stark. "And that was pretty fancy footwork you used on those hombres. Puts me to mind of the way Jorge fights."

"How's that?" Stark's head came quickly about.

"I saw Jorge fight once. He tangled with a couple of

cowpokes who thought he dressed funny." Clete shook his head wonderingly at the memory. "Never seen so much leaping and spinning and whirling by a fellow in all my born days. Feet flying all over the place. Those cowhands never had a chance."

Stark thought of Jorge's steel-toed boots. "Has he ever been to Brazil?"

"Now how in tarnation would I know that?" Clete burst out. Then he frowned with interest. "Why you asking?"

"They have a style of foot-fighting down there. It's called *capoeira*," Stark rolled the word off his tongue. "Sounds like Jorge might've been using that."

"Whatever he used, it sure flattened those poor cowpokes in jig time."

Stark kept his thoughts to himself.

As they neared the B&B, Clete spoke up again. "What'd you make of the widow woman?" His tone carried some of the earlier disapproval he'd shown with Stark for agreeing to a private confab with her.

"The Good Book says something about a stranger who flatters with her words, and who has destroyed many strong men. Reckon that about covers it."

Clete allowed a moment to go by, as though hoping he'd say more. "She make you any sort of an offer?" he asked gruffly at last.

"Yep. I turned her down."

Stark urged Red in front of Clete's mule and dismounted at the barn. He'd said all he intended to say on the subject of Norene Danner.

Chapter Nine

"It's a good six-day run, weather permitting," Brian told Stark. "We'll be making stops at some farms and ranches, one little community that doesn't even have its own store, and a couple of roadhouses." He used a finger to trace their meandering route on the map spread on the kitchen table before them. "We'll be pulling out at first light tomorrow."

"You'll need to use the big wagon," Clete added from where he leaned against the counter. "I'll check it over here shortly. Josh can help me load it this afternoon when his turn as lookout is over."

Brenda turned away from the stove where she was seeing to their noon meal. Ham sizzled in the iron skillet. Sunlight from the window caught her hair and spun it into gold. She didn't quite manage to look boyish in the denims and blue workshirt she wore. A holstered pistol rode her trim waist.

"I hate to have both of you gone for so long," she commented.

Stark tilted his chair back a bit, keeping his boots flat on the floor. The atmosphere in the kitchen of the Langton house was homey and oddly appealing. "We've been gone before," he reminded.

"I know," she acknowledged. "But not for this long." She prodded the ham with a fork, wincing when grease splattered her. "Ouch!"

"We don't have a choice," Brian stated flatly. "We've got to get those deliveries made. Folks are counting on us, and we're already a day late. We've put off making this run for as long as we can."

Brenda moved her hand away from her mouth where she'd pressed the tiny blister. She sighed wistfully. "I suppose you're right."

"Things have been quiet," Stark reminded to allay her fears. "Shouldn't be any trouble while we're gone."

Inwardly he questioned whether that was true. With him and Brian on the trail, the B&B would be more vulnerable than he liked. Over the last couple of weeks he had settled into a routine of riding shotgun on any freight runs that were made. He'd based these tactics on reasoning that hitting a wagon would be easier and less costly in manpower than trying some kind of assault on the forted B&B headquarters itself. But he was also basing his actions on his assessment of the varied passions seething within Norene Danner, and the lengths to which she would go to satisfy them.

There had been no further hostilities following the fracas with her bruisers. Nor had Norene made any effort to renew contact. Stark generally wasn't prey to nerves, but he had to admit that waiting for Norene Danner to make the next move made him uneasy. They were on the defensive, and he knew that was how this game had to be played. But he didn't have to like it.

"Soup's on," Brenda announced. "Clete, would you bless it?"

The ancient mule skinner offered a quick prayer, and Brenda served the meal.

"I'll just take Josh's out to him," she said as the men fell to the ham and potatoes.

"Aw, let him wait," Brian protested. "Won't hurt him none to go hungry."

"Oh, hush." Brenda was out the door and gone before her brother could offer any rejoinder.

She returned shortly to join them. Stark was pleased that she hadn't hung around her beau and distracted him. Not for the first time, he reflected that Jacob Langton had left the B&B in good hands. He hoped he could keep the Widow Danner from taking it out of those hands.

"Reckon I'll see to that wagon," Clete announced, pushing his chair back.

Stark accompanied him. Although he'd ridden shotgun on the other two wagons—the Murphy and a smaller Studebaker—he hadn't done much more than glance at the third vehicle in the B&B fleet.

An old mining wagon of unknown origins, it bulked large under the shed beside the smaller conveyances. Likely it had originally been used to haul machinery to some forgotten mine. The iron tires were wide enough to provide good traction on soft ground, and it looked to be well built and solid. It would, Stark estimated, carry a good four tons, and require eight mules to pull it fully loaded.

A lever brake had been added to the original crude rough lock brake, which was nothing more than a massive hook attached to the body of the wagon by a logging chain. On steep grades the chain would be hooked to a spoke on one of the rear wheels to keep it from turning. Stark was glad for the improvement of the lever brake. The notion of jockeying eight thousand pounds downhill in the old mining wagon with only a single chain holding it in check was an unsettling one. If the chain snapped, being handy with a gun wouldn't do him or anyone else much good.

"Company's coming!" Josh's voice carried from where he perched in the doorway of the hayloft of the barn. A moment later the barking of the two watchdogs confirmed his warning.

Stark and Clete moved out from under the shelter of the shed's roof. Josh peered down at them from the open doors of the hayloft. His rifle was in his hand. "It's the widow woman and those two gaucho gunhands of hers!" he called.

Stark felt a certain grim satisfaction. Maybe now the waiting was over. "Keep an eye peeled out back," he commanded.

He saw Josh nod his understanding, then turn and disappear into the gloom of the loft. Distracting everybody by palavering out front might be just a ploy to let more human wolves slip up unsuspected on the freight headquarters from the rear.

Alerted by the commotion, Brian and Brenda emerged from the house as the visitors arrived. Brenda still wore her gunbelt. Brian toted a rifle. Stark knew better than to waste his breath ordering them back inside where it was safer.

All of the newcomers were mounted. Somehow it didn't surprise Stark to see Norene expertly handling the beautiful steel-gray gelding which pranced beneath her. She wore a black blouse and matching riding skirt, trimmed in the ever-present red. Her fiery hair was done up neatly beneath a flat-brimmed black hat with a red band. Stark noted Brenda self-consciously straightening her own faded shirt, and brushing at her dusty jeans.

Juan was astride his palomino, his saddle bedecked with whip, lasso, and some other strange gear. Jorge's steed was a rangy buckskin.

"That's far enough." Clete's calloused palm nestled on the butt of his huge revolver.

Norene stilled her gelding. She smiled at Stark as if she knew his deepest thoughts, before she ran her glance casually over the others.

"I've got wagons sitting idle and folks hereabouts who won't trade at my store. I'd like to do business with the B&B. Will you invite me in so we can talk?"

"No need for that." Brian squared his shoulders and spoke up. "Say your piece and move on."

She regarded him dismissively, then turned her emerald gaze deliberately on Stark. "Is that right, James?" she purred. "Not even an invitation for coffee? I would've thought you owed me at least that much."

Stark sensed Brenda bristling at the older woman's tone. He wished he was dealing with Juan or Jorge. Or even the devil himself. But then he realized that was probably just what he was doing. "You heard the man," he said aloud.

Norene pursed her lips in a sigh and leaned back provocatively in her saddle. "I'm disappointed. But I do still want to talk business."

"Won't do no good," Brian declared flatly. "We ain't selling out to you."

"I'd make it worth your while." Her gaze slid over Stark. "I'll be generous. I'll pay you twice what this outfit is worth. You'd have plenty to start over elsewhere. You could even have a nice dowry for your little sister there when she finds a man."

Brenda flushed fiercely in rage and humiliation.

"Don't talk like that about her!" Brian snapped. He tilted his rifle so it was leveled at the trio.

Stark saw Juan go suddenly taut. "They're not interested in selling," he said quickly to head off trouble. Now was the wrong time to be slinging lead.

Brian lowered his rifle a bit, maybe understanding how

close he'd come to death. He wouldn't have stood a chance against Juan.

"The executor isn't interested in selling, either," Stark went on. "Now, if that's all you wanted to know, then you've got your answer.

Juan eased up a little. But he was still as dangerous as a coiled rattler.

Norene looked to be enjoying herself. She shifted in the saddle. "Then I'll make another offer. Let's be partners. I'll buy into your operation. Sixty percent, with the agreement that you all still run things."

"No!" Brenda blazed. "We wouldn't go into business with you if our salvation depended on it! Daddy would roll over in his grave!"

"I'd rather hear that from someone with authority," Norene said placidly. Stark was glad Josh wasn't still perched in the hayloft with her under his rifle.

"She speaks for me as well," Brian declared.

Clete rolled his shoulders and spat. "Girlie, I wouldn't work for you on a bet," he drawled.

For the first time Norene's scarlet lips thinned in anger. She recovered almost on the instant and ignored the old man. "What about you, James? Have you given any thought to my offer?"

Stark knew she wasn't talking about the offer she'd just made. And, yeah, he'd thought about it, the way a man thought about an unworthy notion that he couldn't quite shake from his mind. "You see where I'm standing," he told her coolly.

As deliberately as though she was trying out poses for an artist, Norene looked away. She reached up to remove her hat so the long tail of her hair, tied by a black ribbon, fell down past her shoulders. She used one hand to rub the back of her pale neck with a slow circular movement as she gazed off across the landscape.

At last she turned her attention to the Langton siblings. "I do wish you'd think about it." While she spoke, she slid her gaze over to Stark. It seemed to touch him like fire.

He was conscious of Juan's fevered glare. A subtle whisper in his mind tried to tell him he might gain an advantage by playing along with her. But, another voice reminded, a man who lay down with a rattlesnake had to expect to get bitten.

"I've thought about it," he said bluntly. "The answer's no." An image of Prudence flickered before him.

Norene's nostrils flared, but she kept her voice level. "I'm sorry none of you will be reasonable."

She must've passed some unseen signal to Juan, for he swung his head in a casual survey of the B&B holdings. Stark wondered if he noted the tops of the buried cans of coal oil.

Ignoring Stark, Juan fixed his attention on Brian. "Next time you point a rifle in my direction, *niño*, you will not be so lucky as to walk away. And I would not worry about your sister if something should happen to you. She is very pretty. She will have no trouble finding a man. Perhaps I will come and pay court to her myself."

"No, Brian!" Brenda cried before the words were fairly out of the gaucho's mouth.

Brian held himself in check with an effort. The barrel of his rifle trembled but didn't rise. He was smart enough to know he was being baited. "She wouldn't have you," he snarled coldly.

Slowly Stark lowered his hand from where it had hovered over the butt of his .45. He was aware of Clete also relaxing a trifle. Both of them had been primed for action.

Juan and his brother had nerve, he was forced to acknowledge. Against two-to-four odds, counting Brenda, the pair of gauchos had still been willing to risk a showdown.

"Your lucky day, Juan," Stark commented. He glanced at Norene so the gaucho could not mistake his double meaning.

"And maybe your unlucky one, *Señor* Peacemaker." Juan gave a harsh laugh and shifted the palomino a little sidewise. The gear suspended from his saddle clattered and swung with the movement. It drew Stark's eye.

Juan noticed instantly. "Ah, you are maybe familiar with the *boleadoras*," he exclaimed. With his right hand he lifted the collection of leather thongs and iron balls which Stark had noted before hanging from his saddle.

Recognition dawned at last in Stark. "Bolas," he breathed, using the shortened form of the term. His eyes narrowed in calculation.

Juan's odd piece of gear consisted of three leather thongs bound together at one end. At the other end of each was attached an iron ball. The three metal spheres looked like small cannonballs. The weight of the device could be seen in the flex of effort it had taken Juan to lift it one-handed.

The iron balls chimed dully against one another as they swayed in the gaucho's grip. "Maybe I will show you how the bolas works." He hefted the piece higher.

"Juan!" Norene's sharp rebuke froze whatever movement her segundo had begun.

Juan's face clouded with passion. He hesitated, then returned the bolas to his saddle. "Maybe another time, Peacemaker."

"Maybe."

Norene's alabaster features were unreadable. "Good day."

Imperiously she turned her gelding and put the spurs to its steel-gray sides. She kept the reins cruelly tight, making the animal twist and dance beneath her as she quitted the yard. Wordlessly Jorge followed.

Juan bared his teeth in a challenging grin at Stark. No

doubt smarting from the public rebuke by his mistress, he backed the palomino expertly away, so Stark and his companions wouldn't be at his rear. At the gate, he dragged the palomino up onto its back legs, front hooves flailing the air. Snatching his sombrero from his head, he waved it in a mocking salute before pivoting the horse, still on its hind legs. Then, dropping its forefeet to the ground, he raked it with spurs and put it after the retreating shapes of his brother and his employer.

Broodingly Stark watched them go. "That—that witch!" he heard Brenda exclaim with heartfelt emotion, but didn't look around at her.

"Simmer down, sis," Brian soothed, then addressed Stark, "What was that thing he had?"

Stark finally took his attention off the departing riders. "A bolas," he explained. "A weighted throwing rope used by gauchos. An expert can snare all four of the legs of a running horse or steer and bring it down from a lot longer range than a man using a lasso." He mused for a moment then spoke reluctantly. "You might want to give some thought to letting her buy you out. You've got a lot at risk here besides your lives. She won't give up."

"Neither will we!" Brian and Brenda said almost in unison.

Stark grinned.

Chapter Ten

Working by lantern light in the chill predawn darkness, they harnessed the balky mules to the heavily laden mining wagon. The wheels had already been greased, and the tar bucket and water kegs filled. The medicine chest was stocked with calomel, laudanum, and Epsom salts.

The mules snorted and snapped, but submitted meekly enough to the collars. The singletrees were clipped to the doubletrees, and the neck yokes put in place. The biggest pair of mules was selected for the wheelers. Their weight and strength were needed closest to the massive wheels to help the driver control the vehicle on the grades. The middle two spans of animals did the yeoman's work of pulling.

The nimblest and smartest critters were selected for the lead span. It was they, and the left, or nigh, animal in particular who had to respond to the ribbons in the mule skinner's hands, leading the team into turns, and coming to a halt on command. For that nigh animal, Brian had picked Stub, an experienced veteran who had lost part of an ear in some ancient fracas, hence the monicker that had been hung on him.

Brenda shivered and hugged herself, more from apprehension than cold, Stark reckoned, as he and and her brother mounted to the wagon seat at last. Standing at her side, Josh dropped a comforting arm self-consciously across her shoulders.

"Keep your powder dry," Clete advised gruffly.

"Stretch out!" Brian shouted the old command of the wagonmasters, and popped his whip above the heads of the team. Stub gave a twitch of his good ear and surged against the traces. With a rattle of chains and creak of wood, the big wagon lurched forward. Stark braced himself with one palm on the seat as he got the rhythm of its motion. His right hand closed on the lever-action shotgun booted next to the sporting rifle beside him.

Even on smooth ground, sitting a freight wagon was no nap in a downy bed. Stark planted his feet firmly, and let his body move with the jolting motion of the vehicle. He pulled the shotgun and kept it across his knees.

They left Doaksville behind them, emerging from the tangle of woods onto the prairie that covered much of the Indian lands. Brian kept the team to the ruts of the grassy road that snaked across the rolling countryside.

Dawn was turning the horizon golden off to the east. A horseman would make a fine silhouette off that direction, Stark reflected, but the towering shape of the wagon would make an even better one to someone to the west. He had a gut-level dislike of riding on the seat like a sitting target. But he was no stranger to the feeling. As Clete had heard, he'd ridden shotgun before, but he'd never learned to enjoy it.

When the edge of the sun cleared the horizon, casting a spreading golden light before it, he sheathed the shotgun and unshipped his field glasses. The swaying seat of the wagon made an uncertain platform, like a ship on a restless sea, but he surveyed the surrounding terrain as best as he was able. He saw a distant herd of pronghorn antelope, a pair of coyotes returning to their den, and some cowhands headed toward Doaksville, but nothing to alarm him. It didn't make him feel any less of a target.

At his suggestion, Brian had varied the usual route taken on this run. It was the best precaution he could come up with, but, if Norene Danner's hired guns really wanted to find them, he didn't think it would make much difference. Likely they were being followed even now, their pursuers staying off the skyline and biding their time.

With the sun all the way over the horizon, they forded a creek. The road led through the fringe of cottonwoods lining the waterway's course, dropped steeply down, then ascended the bank on the other side. Brian handled the eight-up team like an old hand. The wide wheels found traction in the soft ground, and the mules hauled the lumbering wagon up out of the creek bed.

"You ever hear about the Easterner who came out to these parts to see the sights?" Brian asked. "He came upon a big freight wagon about like this one sunk plumb up to the hubs of its wheels in a mudhole. He looked at the mule skinner and said 'You appear to be in a great deal of trouble.' "

Stark grinned. "And the mule skinner said 'Oh, I'm fine, it's the fellow driving the wagon under mine that's in a heap of trouble,' " he finished the tale.

"You've heard it!" Brian accused.

"Heard it?" Stark echoed. "I was the driver on that second wagon!"

Brian joined him in laughter, but there was a point to the old yarn. Even absent hostile gunmen, freighting was a hazardous business. There were shifting stretches of quicksand along such rivers as the Cimarron that could swallow team, wagon, and mulewhacker without a trace. Dust storms could blind man and beast alike; the sun could blister a fellow near to death, and a blizzard could turn an unseen draw into a death trap.

Brian gave a wondering shake of his head. "Boy howdy, but you've been to see the elephant. Seems like you must've been everywhere and done everything there is to do." His tone was envious.

"I've never done what you're doing," Stark said seriously.

Brian was puzzled. "What's that?"

"Carrying on your pa's business; looking after the rest of your family."

For no good reason that Stark could figure, Prudence came to his mind as he spoke. It didn't make much sense. Even if he was interested in settling down, Prudence sure wasn't the settling down type.

At midmorning they made a stop to allow the mules time for grazing. Animals who'd had a chance to fill their bellies during the day would be more willing to rest at night and not wander off looking for more to eat beyond the ration of grain the mule skinner provided.

By habit, Brian checked over the animals and gear. The midmorning halt was a good time for routine maintenance. But this early in the run, there was little that needed tending to. Stark ascended a nearby ridge with field glasses and the sporting rifle. The dome of the sky was an almost painful turquoise in the cool air. Sharp wisps of cloud darted past from the north high overhead. Down at ground level the breeze was more southerly, rippling across the grass in gentle waves. All of which meant the weather was unsettled, Stark observed with a frown.

Far off, a haze of dust marked drovers moving a herd of horses. The farther out they got in the grasslands, the fewer signs of human activity they'd be seeing, Stark knew. That added up to the fact that what strangers they did see were more likely than not to be hostile.

After lunch they pressed on. Stark took the lines for a spell, threading them between his fingers, keeping a slight tension on them so the critters wouldn't go to loafing or try to turn aside to crop more of the thick buffalo grass. It had been a long while since he'd handled an eight-up team. Stub and a few of the others he knew from past short hauls, but it took him a bit of time to get the feel of all four spans and let them know who was boss.

Gradually he got acquainted with each animal through the reins. The farthest of the two center spans liked to feud with each other, while the left animal of the closer center span pretended to limp in hopes of slowing the pace. A pop of the line against one dusty hip cured him of that for the moment. The right wheeler was the stronger of that pair, and had to be held in a little to let his teammate match him.

Stark took note of each animal's character, working the ribbons accordingly. Soon he had settled into an automatic handling of the team that required little thought. He rocked on the seat with the trundling motion of the heavy vehicle.

Ahead the road passed by one of the odd rocky bluffs that bulged up occasionally from the prairie-like desert islands rising from the sea. Good ambush country, Stark calculated. Best to steer clear. He inclined his head at the sandstone heights and Brian, rifle across his knees, nodded his understanding of the danger. He began to scan the outcroppings with wary eyes.

Stark drew on Stub's line, slacking up on that of the other lead animal. With his head being tugged to the left, Stub stubbornly resisted leaving the familiar road for a moment. Then grudgingly he turned aside. Drawn by the gear connecting them, and with his own guide rein slack, the right animal followed Stub's lead. The whole team slanted off the road. The wagon lurched as it left the ruts, then it was rolling unevenly across the buffalo grass and clods beneath its wide iron wheels.

When they had gone far enough Stark jockeyed the reins, using the right and slacking up on Stub in order to straighten the team's course. The rocky bluff rolled past a couple of hundred yards distant. Brian watched its heights like a hawk.

Once they had swung back onto the road, Stark cast a final glance over his shoulder. He was almost sure it was only his fancy that made him think he detected movement up among the outcroppings.

When they halted to rest the mules in the middle of the afternoon, two hard-faced, gun-hung riders appeared and shouted greetings. Approaching, they drew rein and stared at the shotgun cradled in Stark's arm where he stood near the wagon. Nor did they miss Brian's casual movement to flank them. Mumbling a surly farewell, they rode on, looking for easier pickings. Stark knew they were a fair example of the road agents and stickup artists who had migrated to these lawless lands as the Old West shrunk around them. In a sense, he supposed the same thing had happened to him.

Late in the day they came creaking up to a modest homestead consisting of a sod house and stock shed surrounded by plowed ground. Brian delivered some goods, accepting coin in part payment, and home-canned vegetables in barter to make up the difference. He exchanged pleasantries and news with the weathered farm couple, and slipped some hard candy to their stairstep kids. He took orders for delivery on the next run, and then they headed on their way.

"Good folks," he commented once they were out of earshot.

Stark didn't argue. Despite the evident hardships of their life, the family had seemed happy enough. He questioned whether he had the gumption to make a go of an outfit like that.

They halted at dusk. Brian put a small bell on Stub and turned the mules loose. Stub would stay close, and the other animals wouldn't stray out of the earshot of the bell.

Stark prowled the immediate vicinity of the camp on foot while Brian was rustling up supper. "Expecting trouble tonight?" the youth asked when he tramped back into camp.

"I always expect trouble," Stark told him.

Coyotes yipped and howled back and forth across the darkened grassland as they were finishing their coffee. Nighthawks whispered past overhead.

"I'll take first watch." Stark drained his cup with a final swallow. "You turn in."

The night passed uneventfully. Stark was aware of Brian bringing the mules in before dawn. By daybreak they were on the move.

They rolled up to a roadhouse later that day. Part hostelry, part store, and part tavern, such scattered establishments catered to travelers, cowhands, settlers and desperadoes. A large sod building roofed with grass, dry and dead now in the late fall, housed a dining room, store, bar, and cribs for sleeping. The living quarters of the owners were in the rear. A lean-to shed had been added for storage. A windmill spun in the corral. A few horses nibbled at the hayrack there.

The tough-looking couple who ran the place were pleased to see the heavily laden wagon arrive. In short order, canned foods, durable goods, tools, saddle gear and other odds and ends were transferred from the wagon to the lean-to, and coins and bills were counted out into Brian's hand. A couple of bales of straw were hefted into the wagon to act as packing and help keep the remaining cargo from shifting. In a pinch, it could also be used to feed the team.

Brian introduced the burly owner as Lowrey. He ushered them in for pie his almost equally burly wife had just baked. The dining area was simply a long table for communal meals occupying one end of the large central room. A store counter and goods displayed for sale occupied the other end. A wooden door separated the bar from the rest of the building. It stood partly open. Stark caught the gruff tones of men's voices and the clink of glass against glass. Appeared as though Lowrey had some customers at his bar.

Mrs. Lowrey joined them at the table as they worked on the generous slices of pie. Brian swapped news with the couple while Stark looked on, one ear cocked toward the sounds in the tavern.

"Seen any strangers lately?" Brian queried once with a significant glance at Stark.

Lowrey rubbed whiskered jowls with a big hand. "Nobody special," he advised. "Them four in there look like they could be bad medicine, but I've seen them before. Usually have to end up asking them to ride on when they get too rowdy."

As if to give truth to his words, one man's voice was raised in anger, followed by jeering laughter from his cohorts.

Lowrey scowled darkly. "Looks like it's about that time again." He heaved to his feet, waving a thick arm at Stark who started to join him. "Just keep your seat. They won't give me no trouble. They know if they did, the wouldn't be setting foot in here again. No other whiskey for miles."

He lumbered toward the door, pausing to scoop up the wicked shape of a sawed-off double-barrel shotgun from under the store counter. No trouble was right, Stark mused, not when looking down twin bores in an enclosed space like the sod tavern. Mrs. Lowrey's wide face was unconcerned as she continued to chat with Brian.

Lowrey's voice sounded rumblingly over the complaints

it roused. Movement followed. Stark hitched around in his chair a little bit so his gun was clear of the table, and regarded the doorway steadily.

He tensed as four men shouldered into the room from the bar. The foremost of them was still limping some from the kick Stark had planted on his knee in the main street of Doaksville. He pulled to a sharp halt and let out a curse as he spotted Stark.

The saloon customers were the same four bruisers Norene Danner had sicced on him and Clete. And this time they were all packing iron.

A taut silence fell on them as the rest of them recognized Stark. Mrs. Lowrey stopped talking abruptly. Brian looked sharply about.

Stark figured he was going to have to kill the leader. That worthy cursed again and tossed the bottle he was carrying from right hand to left like he was doing a border shift. The hombre behind him caught his elbow and whispered urgently in his ear, jerking his head to indicate the bulk of the shotgun-toting Lowrey looming in the doorway behind them.

"Come on, let's ride!" one of the others spoke up a little louder than was necessary, and broke away from the group to make for the door.

Grudgingly the leader let himself be persuaded. The others ignored Stark, but the leader kept glaring until he'd hobbled out the door after them.

Lowrey emerged the rest of the way from the tavern. He fingered his sawed-off thoughtfully. "You know them hombres?"

"We've crossed trails," Stark told him dryly. "And I think you're right."

Lowrey's beefy face drew down in puzzlement. "How's that?"

"I think they're bad medicine," Stark answered.

Chapter Eleven

Stark lowered the field glasses and twisted around on the wagon seat. "They're still back there," he reported.

"You figure it's them?" Brian asked. "Been three days since we saw them at Lowrey's place."

Stark couldn't have proven it in one of Prudence's courts of law, but he didn't have many doubts. "It's them."

"What are they waiting for?" Strain tightened Brian's voice. Young and tough he might be, but the notion of the four hard cases dogging their trail throughout the morning hours had plainly begun to fray his nerves.

Stark hitched his shoulders in a noncommittal shrug. "Maybe they're waiting for the right time and place; maybe just keeping an eye on us to report back to the boss lady."

He didn't really believe that last reason himself. He only needed to recall the flaring anger in the eyes of the stove-up leader back at the roadhouse to be sure that, orders or no from Norene, that hombre would be looking to even the score.

More than once during the long morning Stark had been tempted to throw lead back at the quartet of riders dogging their backtrail. But they had persisted in hanging just out of reach of even the high-caliber sporting rifle. And, on the off chance that he was wrong as to their identities, Stark would've hated to accidentally plug some innocent pilgrim from long range. Nor did he cotton to leaving Brian alone long enough to drop back and set up an ambush of his own.

He had first noted their presence early that day, and had been keeping an eye peeled ever since. With the freight route over half finished, most of the deliveries had been made, and the mules no longer had to work as hard at pulling the bulky wagon.

Brian looked to the north. ''Clouds are still building yonder,'' he observed.

Stark nodded grimly. Like a range of mountains off in the distance, a dark rugged mass of storm clouds had been surging up gradually over the horizon as the morning progressed. Where the wagon rumbled along, the sun still shone, and a warmish breeze from the south flattened the grass. All of that was likely to change, Stark calculated bleakly. He recollected Clete's forecast of an early spell of winter. Looked like the ancient teamster had been right.

''Should we stop and let the mules graze?'' Brian asked.

Stark shook his head. ''The wagon's lighter now. Won't hurt them to keep pulling. And there's no point in waiting for our friends back there to catch up. Besides, we need to cover as much ground as we can before that norther hits. Could slow us up considerably when it does.''

Brian gave a nod as though Stark's reasoning confirmed his own. He popped the reins for Stub to pick up the pace a bit. The lead mule flicked his good ear back in irritated response, but complied just the same. The wagon gained a little speed.

The terrain had changed some as they traveled. The rolling grassland had given way to rougher ground, with deep defiles cutting between low steep hillocks. Sandstone and naked red earth showed frequently beneath the clumps of grass studding the slopes. The road was little more than a trace. Bad country to be caught in a blizzard, if that's what was coming down the pike.

Stark feared it was. He took to dividing his time between watching their backtrail for the stalkers and studying the mass of clouds as it loomed higher and higher in the sky.

They had just crested a hogback ridge when the southerly breeze gave an audible sigh, and stopped dead. The black wall of clouds had blotted out half the world now, casting the landscape off to their north under an ominous advancing shadow.

"The wind's turning," Brian said in a low voice.

He reached under the seat for his heavy mackinaw and shrugged into it. Stark found his own sheepskin coat and followed suit, tugging his Stetson down tight atop his ears. At the front of the team, Stub tossed his head and let out an unhappy ear-wracking bray. Brian began maneuvering them toward the shelter of another ridge.

"Looky there," the youngster breathed.

Stark had seen it before, but still he looked. A blue norther was blowing in across the plains all the way from Canada with the velocity of a thousand miles of open country behind it, and they were watching it come.

A far off soughing began to mount to a whistling roar. In the distance the grass suddenly dropped flat as if a giant sheet had been lowered upon it. A grayish wall advanced in its wake.

"Snow," Brian said darkly.

Stark nodded. The snow didn't always make it this far south. When it did, it meant the front was a bearcat.

Now the clouds blotted out the sky and light overhead. The keening of the oncoming wind rose to a scream. Brian drew up the lines and kicked the brake down as they reached the lee side of a low hogback.

"We'll ride it out here!" he had to shout to be heard.

But even the shelter of the ridge didn't help much. The wind tore up its far side and dropped down on them like a hammer, rocking the heavy wagon and staggering the mules in their traces. The corners and edges of the tarp covering the cargo flapped wildly.

Cold enfolded Stark, sucked the air from his lungs. He shifted his shoulder into the wind, turned his collar up with rapidly numbing fingers, and tried to pull his head down like a turtle. That first fierce onslaught of wind still found every inch of his body, cutting through denim and sheepskin and leather with icy blades. Brian, he knew, was faring no better.

He had barely gotten braced when a stinging blast of snowflakes pelted him. In moments the snow was whipping down in flurries so thick it blurred his view of the team in front of the wagon. Yeah, a bearcat for sure. Grimly he set his jaw, hunched his shoulders, and waited for the worst of it to pass.

Finally, after a quarter-hour or so, the first brutal assault of the norther slowed some, but the wind still blew strongly, and the snow continued to fall faster than ever.

"Better get them moving!" Stark hollered. Sitting still with poor shelter in this type of weather was a ticket to frostbite or worse.

Brian skinned on some leather gloves and released the brake. "Yaw, mules!" He popped his whip and the wagon lumbered forward into a snowy purgatory.

The meager road had been all but covered in the first

moments, and things didn't look to be getting any better. Brian drove by feel and instinct and memory. Stark didn't envy him the task.

On all sides of them sight was obscured by a shifting veil of snow through which the shrouded shapes of low hills and ridges loomed in passing. Stark twisted his head about to look back. His face was already numb despite the kerchief he'd pulled up over his nose. His captured breath warmed him some, but its moisture kept the thin fabric on the verge of freezing. Snow blew into his eyes, and he had to blink furiously to clear his vision.

Behind them he could only see their rapidly filling tracks disappear into the snowy haze. Norene Danner's gunhounds were back there somewhere. Had they found shelter, or were they still keeping stubbornly on the trail of their prey? Stark began to wish he'd done more to discourage them. Now nature itself had provided cover from which to attack. Of course, he reminded himself wryly, first they'd have to find their prey which was protected by that same cover.

More than once as the day dragged into the afternoon hours, Stark was given cause to recall Clete's voiced memories of his days in the Pony Express, and to concur with the truth of his words. Of all the weather on the trail, Clete had said, snow was the worst.

And this was more than just snow. It was a full-fledged blizzard. Twisters in the spring, and tree-snapping straight winds in the winter weren't uncommon in these parts. But a blizzard that dropped over a foot of snow in a matter of hours, accompanied by winds that blew it into drifts many times deeper, was a seldom event.

And this one proceeded to do just that. Awareness of time dimmed. There was only the biting snow, the successive shocks of wind, and the cold that penetrated to the heart and lungs and brain. Stark had been accused of having ice water for blood. He felt like that was true at last.

Snow coated the backs of the mules. Brian kept doggedly to driving them. Stark would've offered to spell him, but he didn't know the road like the younger man did. And to blunder off of it into a drift could be fatal. When one of the wide metal wheels did slip into the deeper snow beside the road, Brian jockeyed the reins to get it quickly back onto solid footing.

Stark had slid the sporting rifle into its carrying case and slipped it under the tarp. The shotgun he kept at hand, brushing the snow from it at intervals to keep the mechanism from clogging or freezing up. If he had to use it, his gloves would slow him a little. But he couldn't risk removing them. At these frigid temperatures naked skin would stick to metal in seconds as if held there by glue.

". . . abandoned homestead up ahead." After a coon's age Stark caught the tail end of Brian's announcement. "We can stop there for the night." The wind tore his next words away. ". . . have to spot the turnoff."

The youth said nothing more for an interminable spell before striking at the air angrily with a gloved fist. "Blast! I must've missed it! I'll have to turn around and go back and try to find it. Don't want to stay out in this after dark!"

Stark hadn't been looking forward to that prospect either. Temperatures would plummet once darkness set in, and he was wondering if it was possible to get much colder than he already was. He knew it was possible all right, but not without risking permanent injury from frostbite. Up north he'd seen old-timers lacking fingers and toes from prolonged exposure in blizzards such as this.

Brian worked the reins, but the cold made his movements awkward. He cut the mules in as tight of a circle as he could manage. Stark knew he was relying partly on guesswork as to the borders of the road. Slowly he maneuvered the massive vehicle about. Stark was just set to draw a frigid breath of relief when he felt a jolt as the right rear wheel went off the road and into a drift.

Brian felt it too. Not even bothering to look back, he yelled and worked the whip, hoorawing the spans on. They lunged against the traces in response. Too hard; the increased pull swung the tail of the wagon even further out. The huge metal wheel sank deeper, its weight bearing it down through the drift until the left rear corner of the vehicle tilted up at an alarming angle. Cargo slid and shifted in the bed, throwing more weight to the right, and over the stuck wheel. Already unsettled by the wind and the snow, the team spooked at the sudden lack of response to their efforts. The wagon rocked back and forth as the beasts thrashed in the traces.

With desperate calm Brian plied the ribbons gently until the mules settled down. At last wagon and team sat motionless with one wheel buried up past its hub in the drift.

"Can you feel any bottom under the wheel?" Stark hollered over the wind.

Brian shook his head in the negative. His teeth started to chatter. He clamped his mouth firmly shut.

If the drift wasn't too deep then the mules should be able to work them free once the wide metal tread found purchase on the ground somewhere beneath the snow. But if it sank down too far, the wagon might tip on edge or flip over completely, like a stranded tortoise.

"Let me get back there, then ease them forward, steady-like," Stark managed to form the words with numb lips. He sheathed the shotgun and clambered stiffly down from the seat.

Even on the roadway the snow was up almost over his boots. Stepping high, he slogged to the back of the wagon. The left wheel was still barely in contact with the ground, he saw as he looked things over.

He was careful to stay clear of where he suspected the

edge of the drift lay. The notion of floundering around in snow that could be over his head wasn't appealing. They might not find him until there was a thaw.

He kicked about at the side of the road until he uncovered several large rocks which he jammed under the left wheel. Then he undid one corner of the tarp and fought its flapping in the wind long enough to extract the heavy pry bar they carried for emergencies. Jamming it under the bed, he gave Brian the go-ahead and then heaved up against the levering bar until his boots slipped in the snow beneath him, and the metal bit into the weathered wood of the wagon. The vehicle didn't budge. Stark set his shoulder to it, feeling the heat of his own panting breath against his face. Over the blood pounding in his ears he could hear Brian using whip and voice to urge the mules forward.

"Rock it!" he hollered.

In a moment he felt the wagon lurch as Brian put the mules into a series of alternating halts and lunges. He strained against the pry bar for all he was worth.

It was no good. He could feel the sweat he had raised on his forehead beginning to freeze. Brian slacked off on the mules. Stark relaxed his efforts. He propped his shoulders against the canted side of the wagon, summoning strength for another try. His breath rasped in his lungs.

The startled bray of Stub brought Stark's head up fast. A horse whinnied, and a man's voice shouted a surprised oath. Stark clawed for the .45 beneath his sheekpskin.

Four riders had emerged from the snowy haze ahead of the team. The unexpected encounter had set their horses to shying.

"It's them!" one rider shouted.

"By Godfrey, give it to them!"

Hard on their trail, no doubt hoping to overtake them and attack under cover of the storm, their stalkers had caught up at last. But they'd been expecting to come up on the rear of their quarry, not meet them head-on.

The surprise didn't slow them much. Guns blasted, and muzzle flames speared through the falling snow. Stark went to one knee as he got the Colt clear of its holster. He thought he glimpsed the shadowy form of Brian bailing out of the driver's seat on the far side of the wagon. A bullet chewed wood beside his head. Another rang off the iron wheel like a sledge on an anvil. Then his hand was working the revolver's action with an ease not even the gloves and the cold could dispel, as he thumbed and triggered the .45 in a wrist-jerking barrage that cleared the pistol's cylinder in a pair of seconds.

He heard yells of shock and consternation. He didn't know if he'd scored a hit. Some lead was still coming his way. Dropping, he rolled under the wagon, fumbling for the .38 double-action in the hideout rig at the small of his back. He wriggled forward and, flat on his belly, propped his gunhand on his forearm and began to snap off shots aimed through the haze of snow and powder smoke. A rifle spoke from the far side of the wagon where Brian had disappeared.

"Pull back!" One of the dimly seen riders wheeled his horse to put action to words.

It was enough to decide his cohorts as well. In moments they had faded into the storm from which they had come.

Stark left the final round in the Marlin .38 unfired. He wanted it in reserve, and for the nonce it would take too long to reload. He writhed out from under the wagon and shoved the .45 back into its holster as he came to a wary crouch. Marlin in hand, he legged it at a shambling run to the front of the wagon.

The mules were all het up in the traces. Their plungings made the wagon rock. Stark reached to yank the lever-action shotgun from its sheath with a savage satisfaction.

A man riding shotgun wasn't much good without his weapon.

Unhurt, Brian appeared and clambered on to the seat, taking the reins to try to settle the mules. In moments his sure hand had gotten them calmed, and Stark had both pistols reloaded. He thumbed buckshot loads from his bandolier and crammed them into his coat pockets.

"They'll be coming at us again." Stark had do doubts about the words he uttered. Regrouped and knowing what awaited them, the hard cases would be even more dangerous now. "They'll spread out and hit us from three sides," he went on, voicing his conclusions aloud. None of the attackers would want to risk getting trapped in the drift. "The wagon will give us some cover. Take the tarp off and we'll get in the back."

Brian fell to obeying his command. Stark held the shotgun at the ready, probing the storm with narrowed eyes, as the younger man worked. The tarp came loose and flapped away in the wind like a giant vulture. They'd recover it later or use the spare, Stark reckoned grimly, provided they survived the coming fracas.

He had to figure all four of the gunmen would be mounting the attack. For the amount of lead he'd thrown, he didn't think he'd so much as winged one of them. Snow was beginning to collect on him. He didn't bother to brush it off. Its presence was a plus. It would make him harder to see.

Brian scrambled into the bed and propped his rifle barrel on the side. "I'll cover you," he advised tersely.

The kid was handling himself like a pro. Stark joined him in the back of the wagon. The sides were thick enough to stop most slugs. They reached to Stark's chest. The wagon made a pretty fair fort.

Stark squinted into the snow, trying to pierce the veil. He levered a shell into the breech of the shotgun. A couple of times he glanced over his shoulder, hoping he had been right in thinking that the gunmen wouldn't risk attacking across the treacherous drift.

There was no warning. The snow muffled the hooves of their mounts. They appeared like phantom centaurs, taking form and substance out of the storm itself, converging on the wagon in a wide arc just as Stark had forecast. Three handguns were spitting lead. The fourth fellow was managing to trigger a rifle as he charged. The gunfire mingled with their wild barbaric yells.

Stark concentrated on the two bearing in from the left. He pressed the shotgun's butt to his shoulder, lined it roughly on the nearest figure, and pulled the trigger. It was like a cannon firing grapeshot. The widening charge rent the shroud of the storm and tore his target, somersaulting him backwards out of the saddle.

A rifle bullet sang past Stark's ear. The mounted rifleman was good with his piece. Stark shifted aim, blinking the snow from his eyes, and fired. A solid load this time, and it missed. The rider let out a cougar's yell and cut loose with his rifle again. He was in close now, close enough so Stark barely had to aim at all to catch him with the wad of buckshot in the next shell. The horse veered frantically away as its owner was swatted from its back.

The mules were braying. The wagon rocked beneath Stark's feet at their antics. Brian's rifle blasted. Stark swiveled at the waist. Brian had dropped one of his targets, but the other was almost upon them, pistol extended to fire point-blank as Brian fumbled desperately to reload his rifle.

The boom of the shotgun eclipsed the rest of the racket. This time Stark didn't miss with the solid load. The attacker tumbled into the snow with a cry, and his horse, unable to swerve, rebounded off the side of the wagon with a jolting impact.

Beneath Stark's boots he felt the wagon start to move.

He realized that the mules' panicked efforts to flee the gun-fight, coupled with the collision by the horse, had achieved what they'd been unable to manage before. The left rear wheel bit in and the right wheel clawed itself up out of the drift. Brian dived for the reins as the team lurched forward in a run.

In a trice he had them slowed. The bulky wagon lumbered to a halt. Stark cast a glance at their backtrail. Four fallen shapes were already starting to disappear under a shroud of snow.

He gave his head a wondering shake. "Guess that's one way of getting the wagon loose."

Chapter Twelve

"Would you please state your name for the witnesses?" Prudence McKay requested.

"Elmer Dansfield," the elderly man seated across from her at the conference table responded promptly.

"Is this your Last Will and Testament?" Prudence indicated the papers before him.

"I reckon it is. You ought to know. You done wrote it up for me."

"Yes, I know, Mr. Dansfield, but you need to state this for the witnesses," Prudence explained patiently.

"Oh." Her client glanced at the two bank clerks she had conscripted to act as witnesses. "I savvy. Yep, fellows, it's my will."

"Very good. Now, have you read the will and are you satisfied with it?"

"Yes, ma'am," he obliged her by answering without comment.

"Would you like for these gentlemen to witness your signing of it?"

"Well, if they're willing."

"And are you signing it of your own free will?"

"Nobody's got a pistol pointed at me, if that's what you mean."

"You're not being forced to sign it. Is that correct?"

"Yep, for a fact."

Prudence heaved a mental sigh of relief as he scrawled his name and the witnesses added theirs. The formalities necessary for executing a will were just silly enough to arouse confusion, anger, or humor even in her more sophisticated and well-educated clients. Elmer Dansfield was neither of these, for all his being a kindly and good-hearted man with the foresight to provide for his wife and children.

In many ways he reminded her of Jacob Langton who had signed his will in the same setting, she reflected as she strode briskly along the bustling sidewalks, briefcase in hand, to return to her office. A shawl draped over the shoulders of her dark blue dress was enough to ward off the day's coolness, although she had to step carefully to avoid the puddles and occasional sludge which were all that remained of the freak fall blizzard that had swept the territory barely a week before. With the typical vagaries of the weather in Oklahoma Territory, the blizzard had been followed by a few days of warmer temperatures and bright sunshine. That had been enough to melt a good deal of the snow, and enable the shopkeepers to clear the sidewalks fronting their stores.

Although she had gotten verification from the court in South McAlister that the documents in the Langton estate had been filed, she had received no word from her clients or James Stark, beyond a brief impersonal letter from him advising that they had arrived safely. After that, there had been only silence.

She wasn't sure whether she should feel relieved or piqued. On the one hand, the silence, in all likelihood, meant that there had been no major problems. On the other, to be all but ignored by the man, particularly when he was in her employ, was all but insufferable. This was especially so in light of the performance she had put on at the train station as he was leaving.

She had, she knew, quite deliberately used her feminine charms to soothe over a potential rift with Stark, which, in all honesty, might've been partly her fault. She supposed she could've been more diplomatic in asking him to protect the Langton holdings.

But her scheme to deflect his anger had worked so well that, even now, it brought a mingled flush of pleasure and satisfaction to her face. Still, she chided herself, familiar as she was in competing in a man's world, it was not a tactic she would've used quite so blatantly on any other male. In fact she felt a little guilty for having done so on Stark.

What made James Stark different? Why had she actually *enjoyed* the calculated flirtation with him, when she generally considered such things beneath her professional dignity? Certainly she and James had more than a business relationship. But, attractive though he was, she knew that their relationship could never go beyond mere friendship. His violent lifestyle made anything else unthinkable.

Had she herself now been the one to finally take it beyond friendship? she questioned suddenly. What would she have done if he had actually followed through with the intent to to embrace her that she was sure she had read in his eyes? And, a mischievous voice pestered, hadn't she in some secret part of herself, actually welcomed the opportunity to flirt with him? What did that say about her true feelings for him, feelings she had no desire to uncover?

Did she?

Thankfully her arrival at her office put an end to such

unsettling questions. She had barely gotten seated behind her desk, ready to pitch into the morning's paperwork, when someone entered her outer office.

Rising, she crossed to the doorway. "Yes?" she inquired, then halted to study the newcomer who was swaggering toward her.

The man—youth?—was almost a stereotype of how the Eastern dime novelists expected a young Western gunfighter to look. He was dressed all in black tight-fitting clothes—shirt, vest and pants. High-heeled riding boots gleamed so brightly they almost hurt her eyes. His thumbs were hooked in the tooled gunbelt encircling his lean hips. A black Stetson studded with silver chochos was tilted rakishly back above a thin face that was handsome enough to be called pretty.

The most curious aspect of him, however, was the way he wore his pearl-handled pistol slanted in its holster across his lower belly. Prudence had been around Stark enough to realize that such positioning might give a gunman a faint edge in speed. Provided, that is, she reflected wryly, he could avoid putting a hole in himself during such mundane activities as, say, walking, sitting, or bending over.

"May I help you?" she asked

He halted and made a show of rocking back and forth on the high heels of his boots. Probably practiced in front of a mirror, she decided. He seemed to be giving her a chance to admire his manliness, but he was slight in build, and not a great deal taller than she was herself.

"Why, maybe you can, little miss," he got around at last to answering her query. "Would you be the lady lawyer?" His eyes gleamed with appreciation of her tiny shapely figure. Maybe his pause had been to give him a chance to admire her.

"I'm Prudence McKay," she confirmed coolly. Privately

she hoped he wasn't wanting her to represent him in some legal capacity.

"I understand you're handling—" He paused as though to remember some phrase in which he'd been carefully coached—"the estate of Jacob Langton."

A wariness settled on Prudence like the shawl she had just removed. "I'm the named executor of the estate," she conceded.

"Mighty glad to hear it." He smiled a triumphant smile that made her of a sudden stop thinking of him as a fool, and instead regard him as a poisonous centipede.

"I'm known as the Konowa Kid," he went on. "Never been much for a last name, but I reckon if I had one, it would have to be Langton, seeing as how I'm the illegitimate son of Jacob Langton, may he rest in peace!"

"What?" Prudence gasped.

The so-called Konowa Kid was nodding with a sneering pride. "That's right. The old scoundrel had a kid on the wrong side of the blanket, and I've come to claim my rightful share of his estate."

"Your identity will have to be established in a court of law," Prudence said automatically. Could his claim be true? she asked herself. She could see no trace of the Jacob Langton she had briefly known, in the arrogant dissolute youth before her. And Jacob Langton had not impressed her as a man given to immorality. But stranger things had happened. . . .

"I'll do whatever it takes to get what's coming to me," the Kid asserted boldly.

Prudence had a notion of what she'd like for him to have coming, but she kept her face composed. "Step into my office, please." She put her desk between them as he strutted on in to the next room. "Sit down."

He complied, stretching his skinny legs listlessly out in

front of him. "Maybe you've heard of me?" he probed
hopefully.

Aspiring gunfighters like him were a dime a dozen in
these parts, but something about his odd holster and his
feline movements made her think he might be more dangerous than most. "No, your name hasn't come up," she
answered his question aloud.

He masked only some of his disappointment at her
denial.

She wrote his sobriquet on a clean pad and poised her
pen, fixing him with her best intimidating courtroom stare
until he began to shift uncomfortably.

"Who is your mother?" she asked crisply.

"Name of Miranda Callan."

"Will she confirm your claim?"

"She won't confirm nothing, seeing as how she's dead.
The pox got her a couple of months back. She was working
at a saloon over to Violet Springs."

That disreputable trouble town was a cesspool of iniquity
on the border known as Hell's Fringe between Oklahoma
Territory and the Indian lands. Any woman working there
would certainly be at risk of just such a death. "Do you
have any proof that Jacob Langton was your father?"

"Just what my mama told me before she died."

"And that was?"

Prudence listened and jotted a few notes as he recounted
a sordid tale of a family man spending his money on a
saloon girl, then leaving her high and dry in the family
way.

"Did she ever try to get in touch with him after you
were born?"

"Wouldn't know about that. Like I told you, she kept it
a secret from me until she was on her deathbed."

"Is there anyone who could confirm her relationship
with him?"

"You mean confirm that the sorry beggar got her with child and then hightailed it?" he snapped.

"If that's your story."

"Why, I reckon we—I mean, I—could scrounge up some witnesses."

Or buy them, Prudence added cynically to herself. She was liking this less and less. The Konowa Kid impressed her as someone who'd been hired to play a role. She was virtually certain she could disprove his assertions. But by making his claim in court, he could certainly delay the probate process and create problems for Jacob Langton's real heirs.

"How did you learn of Jacob Langton's death?" she continued to probe.

"Well, when I got word my poor ma was dying, I went to see her," he began as though reciting a memorized speech.

"Where were you when you learned she was sick?" Prudence cut in quickly before he could get too far into his performance.

It threw him a little. "I was in the Indian lands," he answered.

"Do you live in Indian Territory?"

"You might say I live pretty much where I please." He squared his narrow shoulders and jutted his delicate chin as he spoke. At last, Prudence sensed, she might be hearing some honesty out of him, and all by virtue of employing the time-tested ploy of getting a man to talk about himself. "I been on my own a good spell now, making my way with this." He dropped slender fingers to caress the pearl butt of his oddly slung revolver.

"Oh?" Prudence responded without inflection. "You're a lawman then?"

The Kid sneered. "Naw, I don't sell my gun for peanuts like them lawdogs do. I draw top dollar for my services."

So he was nothing more than a cheap hired gun, as she had first suspected, Prudence concluded with satisfaction. It didn't make him a liar, but, to her mind, it made his tale just that much more suspect.

"Speaking of fast guns and such," the Kid continued. "I understand you're mighty close to James Stark, the one who calls himself the Peacemaker." His leer made no secret of what he believed about her relationship with Stark.

Prudence drew herself up stiffly. "We're friends . . . and business associates." She hated the way her voice faltered a bit. "What concern is it of yours?" She made her tone cold.

"I've always wondered if he was as good as they say. Word is, he's the fastest man with a gun in these parts. Me, I've always figured I'm faster. Let me tell you, honey, I'm greased lightning when it comes to getting this baby out, especially wearing it the way I do." He patted the pistol lovingly. "Truth is, I been hankering to try Stark out, man-to-man, gun-to-gun."

Prudence regarded him contemptuously. She spoke without thinking. "You'd be a fool to challenge him. No one can beat Jim with a gun."

With sudden horror she realized she had bragged on Stark's skill with a gun, and, worse, had actually felt a fierce surge of pride over the thing she objected to most about him. What in heaven's name was wrong with her?

The Kid's eyes had narrowed. He didn't appear to have noticed her mortification. "A fool, huh?" he snapped. "Maybe one day we'll be seeing about that."

"You were telling me how you came to learn of Jacob Langton's death," Prudence reminded as she regained her composure.

The Kid shifted around like a snake in his chair. "Reckon you got a right to be worried about your man," he boasted. "But, like I was saying, after my ma passed on, I headed to Doaksville where she told me pa lived. Wasn't until I got there that I learned he'd up and died."

"How did you get my name?"

"I asked around town and found out he owned a nice freight company. Then I got to talking to the lady who runs the saloon." Strangely, he licked his lips as if over some lascivious memory. "She told me to come see you about making a claim for my share of his outfit." His face took on an unpleasant lecherous cast. "Now that I've seen you, I'm plumb glad I made the trip. James Stark is a mighty lucky man."

Prudence tried to ignore his unwholesome gaze and comments. "You spoke with Norene Danner?"

The Kid nodded emphatically. "Yes, ma'am, I did. And let me tell you that, until I seen you, she was the nicest-looking thing I've seen come down the pike in a long while. Yessir, nice-looking. All that fine red hair. But, ma'am, I got to say you're every bit as fine as she is!"

Prudence groped numbly for comprehension. "What are you talking about?"

"Why, ma'am, I'm paying you a compliment."

"Are you telling me that Mrs. Danner is not an elderly woman?" It took an effort for her to phrase the question.

"Elderly? You mean old? Shoot, no! She's ripe as a spring peach, if you know what I mean, and I got a hunch you do. When I heard a widow woman was running things in town, I expected her to be some old hag. But I'm here to tell you, that sure ain't the case!"

Apparently his expectations and hers had not been too different, Prudence mused behind her composed features. An unworthy thought flashed across her mind. Jim Stark cut a handsome figure of a man. Could this—this widow have somehow beguiled him? Was that why there had been no word from him for so long?

She gave a mental shake of her head. Foolish thoughts.

Jim could take care of himself. He encountered attractive women frequently here in the cosmopolitan society of Guthrie, and hadn't lost his head to any of them. And what difference should it make to her anyway? She had no interest in him beyond friendship.

But, she reasoned rapidly, she did have an interest in this case, as the executor of Jacob Langton's estate. The unexpected arrival of this Konowa Kid on the scene was certainly a matter of significance to Jacob Langton's heirs.

"You've shown me nothing to verify your claim," she told her visitor firmly. "I'm sorry, but your word is not enough to entitle you to a share in the estate. I would recommend that you employ an attorney to represent you. If you or he wish to provide me with documentation or other proof, I will certainly consider it. At any rate, your attorney will be able to present your claim in the appropriate fashion, once the estate is opened. For now, I'm quite busy. Good day." She occupied herself with the papers on her desk.

Her manner forestalled any immediate protest from him. She heard him get up and cross to the door. He paused. "You tell your sweetheart I'll be looking for him. Then I'll show you who's the better man."

Prudence didn't lift her gaze until his footsteps departed the outer office. She hadn't focused on a single bit of the paperwork on her desk.

The news of the Konowa Kid's appearance was far too important to trust to the mail or telegraph, she decided resolutely. She needed to go to Doaksville personally to advise the Langton children of this development, and to see how the affairs of the estate were being handled. Her other cases could wait. She would begin to pack immediately.

As she bustled about closing the office, she did her best to banish the images of James Stark that persisted in flickering through her mind.

Chapter Thirteen

Stark looked up from the workbench as a slight figure darkened the barn doorway.

"Oh, I'm sorry, Mr. Stark," Josh apologized hurriedly. "I was just coming to mend a harness I noticed needed some work." He broke off in puzzlement as his eye fell on the collection of stones and leather thongs in front of Stark on the bench. "What's that?"

"I'm fixing to test a notion of mine," Stark answered, rising from where he straddled the bench. The cocoon had finally opened and his idea had emerged. "Come on," he invited. "Bring the bucket." He strode toward the rear doorway of the barn, his creation in his fist. "Was there much cover alongside the road where Mr. Langton died?"

"There were some trees and underbrush."

Stark nodded at the confirmation. "Set the bucket on the post yonder," he ordered as the youth emerged behind him into the corral.

While Josh complied, Stark shook the weighted cords out

117

until they dangled at his side. He hefted them musingly. He had taken three leather thongs, tied their ends together, then bound stones of roughly equal size and weight to the other ends of the cords. It was pretty crude, he admitted to himself, but it might do the trick just the same.

Josh rejoined him, watching expectantly as Stark swung the device over his head and began to whirl it in faster and faster circles, the stones whistling through the air. Stark had never thrown one of these before. He judged the distance, relying on experience with lasso and whip to gauge the moment of release. His arm snapped forward, and his makeshift bolas spun through the air.

He got lucky on his first throw. The weighted whirling ropes encircled the bucket like a fistful of flung snakes. Stark heard the clang of rock meeting metal, although by that time the thongs and stones were moving so fast he couldn't see the impact. Enveloped in leather and stones, the bucket sailed off its perch atop the post.

Josh ran to retrieve the pail. Stark nodded bleakly to himself. The whirling thongs, weighted by the stones, packed a lot of power. Even before Josh returned with the bolas and battered bucket, Stark was sure he had his answer. He knew how Jacob Langton and Old Man Danner had been killed. An expert throw of a bolas from cover could've resulted in just such injuries as both of them had received.

"Company coming," Clete announced from the hayloft. "You better have a look."

Passing back through the barn, Stark tossed the crude throwing rope into a darkened corner. As he emerged he saw the watchdogs racing the wheels of an approaching buckboard. He drew in his breath sharply as he got a look at its occupants.

Even after what must've been a tiring dusty trip by rail and buckboard, Prudence McKay still managed to look fresh and attractive where she sat beside the buckboard's driver. As she saw Stark, she stiffened and half rose to her feet in the unsteady conveyance. Then, bracing herself with a palm, she sank back down. Stark couldn't read her expression. He wondered what his own looked like. He felt a tightness in his chest and didn't know why.

"Howdy, Stark," the driver greeted in slightly accented English. He gave a hard grin beneath a full dark mustache. A U.S. deputy marshal's badge gleamed on his vest, partly hidden by his jacket.

Stark knew and respected the badge's owner. Born in Denmark, Chris Madsen had fought in the Franco-Prussian War and served in the French Foreign Legion, before ever coming to America, where he had been an Indian scout for the cavalry until joining the law enforcement effort in Oklahoma Territory. Known for his skill with firearms and his even temperament, he was a bad man to cross, but a good one to have siding you.

"This nice-looking barrister tracked me down in South McAlister and convinced me she needed to see you. So, here she is," Madsen explained once he'd brought the buckboard to a halt.

Stark found himself striding forward. Prudence slipped easily from the wagon seat to meet him, and he had to draw up short to keep from colliding with her. She lifted her hand in that familiar fleeting touch on his chest, part greeting, part restraint. He could see relief mingled with concern in her eyes.

"What are you doing here?" His query sounded harsher than he had intended, and she flinched back a little.

"I've got news. It's important." She looked to be ready to add more, but the sudden arrival of Brenda and her brother forestalled her. The pair drew her quickly aside, their voices rising in excited greetings.

Madsen propped a forearm on his knee and cocked his

head inquiringly. Stark knew he hadn't missed Clete's armed presence on sentry duty in the hayloft.

"Obliged for your bringing her," Stark offered.

"No trouble. She said it was mighty important, and I hadn't been over this way for a spell. Neither have any of the other deputies, so far as I know."

"Reckon not," Stark agreed.

"You got trouble hereabouts?" Madsen's voice tightened as he asked the question.

Stark gave it a second's calculation before he answered. Limited by numbers and jurisdiction, the U.S. deputies were few and far between in the Indian lands. He didn't yet have anything he wanted to give Madsen. There were still too many questions, and too many matters that he wanted to deal with himself.

"Nothing I can't handle," he told Madsen. "If it gets to where I need you, I'll give you a holler."

"I'll hold you to that." Madsen kicked off the brake preparatory to leaving.

Stark frowned and tossed his head at Prudence. "What about her?"

Madsen grinned. "She says she's staying."

"That's loco!"

"Maybe so, but I ain't going to argue with her!" He sawed the lines to bring the wagon about.

Stark wheeled to see that the Langton kids were already escorting Prudence toward the house. Brian was toting her valise. He caught Prudence's face turned briefly toward him before she entered the house.

"Don't worry," Clete's voice drawled from where he had been observing in the hayloft. "We'll make a fine mule skinner out of her!"

"You might be surprised," Stark growled and marched after the others.

Over coffee, Prudence shared the reason for her visit.

She was certain, she concluded, that the so-called Konowa Kid would be showing up soon in Doaksville.

"I don't believe his story!" Brenda proclaimed fiercely. "It's all a bunch of lies! Daddy wouldn't have done that!"

Brian nodded emphatically in agreement. His jaw was set stiffly.

"Tell me what's been happening here," Prudence urged.

Both kids looked with expectation at Stark where he stood leaning against the kitchen wall, arms folded across his chest. Keeping it short, he related the events of the past few weeks, a little surprised at Prudence's lack of questions. She seemed preoccupied with something else. He reasoned it was dissatisfaction with all the fighting and killing that had gone on in her absence. But she'd hired him as a troubleshooter. What the deuce had she expected him to do?

"Did you meet with this woman, Norene Danner?" she queried almost sharply once he was finished.

"Yep," Stark affirmed laconically.

"What did she want?" A faint flush rose to Prudence's face.

Stark repeated the offers Norene had made to purchase the B&B. Something told him to skip over the proposal to him.

"That's all?" Prudence demanded when he finished.

Stark shifted his shoulders to get more comfortable. "She offered to hire me," he temporized.

For a moment Prudence brooded. "I need to meet her," she announced at last.

Stark straightened away from the wall. "That's fool talk!" he announced bluntly.

"Why?" she flared with an intensity that surprised him.

"Her saloon's no place for you," he found an answer. "Could be dangerous."

"Is that where you met with her?"

"Once."

"I've been in dangerous places before."

Stark shook his head. "Doesn't matter. You don't need to be going to see her."

"It's part of my job as executor to meet with anyone interested in the estate!" she asserted.

"You're not executrix until the court appoints you," Stark reminded coldly. Deliberately he used the feminine form of the title.

Her full lips thinned. She stood up, her back as rigid as a branding iron. "You may accompany me if you wish," she stated. "I'm going."

"Now?" Stark blurted.

"Do you have a better time?"

There was no gainsaying her. Stark knew when he was whipsawed. He couldn't let her go on her own, and he had no doubt that she was going. "Hitch up a team, Josh," he ordered tightly.

They waited in tense silence, broken only by the rapid tapping of Prudence's foot. It halted when she glanced down as if discovering the offending member for the first time, and stilled it with a visible effort. Stark's face was stony.

She sat tautly beside him on the seat as the wagon jolted into town. Once, when a wheel hit a pothole, she was thrown against him. For an instant he felt her softness and caught the sweet scent of her. She drew hurriedly away and he fancied she cast a quick sidewards glance at him. He kept his eyes straight ahead.

When they halted in front of the Crimson Lady, he imagined he detected the first traces of misgivings in her. She gazed up at the provocative portrait adorning the billboard.

"That's her, isn't it?" she asked with sudden intuition.

"Yeah. Pretty good likeness too."

Her firm little jaw tightened. "Let's go in."

"No second thoughts?"

"None."

Stark gave a single shake of his head. "Don't say you didn't get fair warning."

She didn't answer, but descended gracefully from the wagon before he had a chance to offer a hand. For a pair of seconds she stood on the boardwalk, seeming to gather her resolve. She had taken time at the house to freshen up, and Stark mused that the reflection she cast in the window of the saloon was a fetching one. With her dusky hair swept up, her petite figure displayed by her modest dress, she looked lovely and feminine and very determined.

Stark drew a deep breath and mounted the boardwalk. He went in ahead of her, foregoing his manners to get the first look at the layout. At this hour of the afternoon there was a motley collection of rowdies, lowlifes and cowpokes occupying the barroom.

The appearance of Prudence in the decadent surroundings drew some unwholesome attention. She stayed close beside Stark, but there was no evidence of fear or hesitation in her bearing, he noted without surprise.

A familiar imposing figure rose swiftly from a table where a half-dozen hard cases were seated. Stark reckoned them to be on Norene's payroll. They watched with jaded interest as their segundo halted in front of the newcomers.

"Ah, the Peacemaker and a lovely *señorita*," Juan's greeting was gracious, but his hot eyes were devouring her trim form like a pampas hawk diving on a sparrow.

"Tell your boss I'm here with Miss McKay from Guthrie to see her," Stark ordered.

Juan's face clouded at his tone, but after a hesitation he jerked his head at the barkeep. "Tell her."

The minion headed for the door to the back of the building.

"Let me buy you and the lady a drink," Juan invited, moving to the bar.

"We'll pass," Stark answered, but he drifted toward the bar nonetheless. From there he could keep an eye on the whole room. Jorge, Juan's brother, didn't seem to be present, he noted.

Juan circled behind the bar as if he owned the joint, produced a bottle and poured himself a shot. He gave an inquiring look at Stark and Prudence. When neither responded he shrugged and lifted the glass toward Prudence.

"To the Peacemaker's lovely lady." His lecherous features were alight with his desires.

For the first time Prudence shrank a little closer to Stark. He didn't blame her.

Juan threw the drink down in a single gulp, wiped the back of a calloused hand across his mouth and studied Spark speculatively.

"What happened to them, hombre?" he asked softly. "There were four of them, and none of them came back."

"You missing some of your crew?" Stark queried carelessly. "Now that there's been a thaw, maybe they'll show up." At least that hadn't been his own fate, he mused with grim thankfulness.

"What did you use on them?" Juan's voice was as soft and deceptive as the whisper of a rattler's scales on sandstone.

Stark was conscious of Prudence's strained presence beside him. He didn't cotton to this sort of talk with her nearby, but he wouldn't crawfish for the big gaucho. "We got us a saying in these parts."

"And what is that?"

"Buckshot means burying. Might pay for you to remember it."

Juan didn't understand for a handful of seconds. Then he grinned with cold menace. "I will remember it." He poured himself another drink and some of his affability returned. "You know, Peacemaker, I think you would make a good gaucho."

"Maybe some day you'll get the chance to find out."

"Soon," Juan promised, and downed the second drink.

He conjured an enormous cigar with a flourish, and got it going. He puffed with great satisfaction until smoke hung over the bar like the aftermath of a shoot-out. Prudence wrinkled her pert nose with displeasure. Juan saw and smiled around the stogie with wicked pleasure. Wordlessly he came up with a twin to the first cigar and proffered it to Stark, eyebrows raised in inquiry. Stark shook his head. Juan's smile widened.

The barkeep reappeared. "Mrs. Danner says she'll see you in her office," he growled and turned to lead the way.

Prudence followed without a glance or word at Juan.

"Hey," the gaucho said softly as Stark swung about to follow.

Stark paused. "Yeah?"

"Maybe you would like my bolas to rope and tie that one," he suggested.

"Don't think it would hold her," Stark answered, getting a chuckle out of Juan. "Besides," he added, "She might use it on me. I could end up with a broke neck and busted skull."

Juan's laughter cut off abruptly. Stark felt the man's burning eyes on his back as he followed Prudence into Norene's lair.

Chapter Fourteen

S tark felt a twinge of relief when the barkeep stopped at a door opposite that of Norene's private chambers. The notion of Prudence in that lavish decadence didn't set well with him.

The barkeep knocked at the door, and without waiting for a response, brushed past Stark and headed back down the hallway. Prudence stood with head up and shoulders squared beneath the fabric of her dark dress. Stark shifted his feet, then reached impatiently for the knob. The panel swung open before his fingers could close on it.

"Come in." Stunning in a red gown that left her pearly shoulders bare, Norene Danner stepped back and gestured them inside. Her hair was done in a casual upsweep that displayed her smooth neck and only emphasized the bareness of her shoulders. A jade pendant hung just above the neckline of her dress.

All but ignoring Stark, she drew back to regard Prudence boldly from head to toe. "James," she said to him then.

126

"You do have good taste. If I was a man I might like her myself."

Prudence bristled like a goaded bobcat. "I don't think I'd be your type, *Mrs.* Danner. It's a pleasure to meet you at last. I'm Prudence McKay. You have such a nice saloon. The painting outside doesn't do you justice."

"You're sweet to say so." Norene reached to close the door, managing to come between Stark and Prudence as she did so. Stark felt the brush of her body against his. When she turned back to Prudence, her smile was acid. "You'll have to see the full portrait of me in my chambers. Jim certainly found it . . . interesting."

Stark couldn't quite hide his involuntary wince. Prudence looked at him sharply, her eyes narrowed and questioning.

"Won't you sit down?" Norene radiated a subdued glee at her victory in that first scathing exchange.

Stark finally took in the details of what was obviously a man's office. Fine paneling covered the walls. The furniture was oak and massively built. A custom Winchester of some sort was mounted behind the hand-carved desk. Only a colorful spray of imported peacock feathers in a corner marred the heavy masculinity of the room.

Plainly this must've been her late husband's office, Stark speculated. For reasons of her own, she had chosen to leave it virtually unchanged, although there was no doubt she considered herself in charge here.

At her invite, they took the solid straightback chairs in front of the wide desk. Rounding it, Norene stood for a moment, posing as if once more on the stage in Chicago. Then she sank into the leather swivel chair with a languid grace. She drew a deep breath that made Stark look quickly away. He fancied he could still see fur hanging in the air from that opening exchange.

"Well, now, Pru," Norene broke off her words. "I can call you that, can't I?"

"I prefer Miss McKay," Prudence said stiffly.

"Of course. Well, as I was about to say, I'm sure we can come to some sort of an agreement or understanding about the B&B."

"I don't think so."

"Why ever not? It's obviously ridiculous to think of those children running it, and I'm willing to make them a fair deal."

"You're wasting your time, Mrs. Danner."

Norene coiled back in her chair and regarded Prudence from hooded emerald eyes. "I don't know why you're being unreasonable. After all, we're both women who operate successfully in a man's world of business affairs."

"The difference is," Prudence came back, "I earned what I have."

Red flames leaped in the jade depths of Norene's eyes. "Oh, I earned what I have, too, honey," she said vehemently. "Don't ever think I didn't."

"I guess the real difference is in the way we earned it." Prudence locked her gaze with that of Norene.

For long seconds, that dragged like cat's claws hung in thick fabric, the two women stared at each other across the desk. At last Norene's full lips curled in a smile that was almost scornful.

"I do believe you are right," she conceded slowly. "We can't work together after all."

"Then we understand each other." Prudence rose abruptly to her feet.

Belatedly Stark followed suit. He figured the meeting— or whatever this had been—was over.

But Prudence wasn't quite done yet. "I'd advise you to quit trying to take what doesn't belong to you."

Norene leaned back lazily once more. "I think ownership of the property is still open to question."

Prudence hesitated for just a beat. "No," she said flatly then. "There's no question at all."

Norene smiled triumphantly at her hesitation. "Isn't there?"

Prudence turned sharply on her heel and took Stark's arm. Her fingers gripped with surprising strength. "Come on, Jim."

Stark let himself be towed out the door. The last glimpse he had of Norene, she was still smiling like a satisfied cat. He was glad to get out of the place and shut the door behind them.

Prudence hissed something under her breath.

"What?" Stark said in surprise.

"Nothing!" She released his arm as if it had suddenly turned red-hot, and marched off down the hall.

Stark shook his head, threw one last glance at the door, then followed her. He seemed to be doing that a lot lately, he thought with irritation.

As they reentered the barroom he noted automatically that Juan was nowhere in sight. He wasn't sure he liked that, but he had no time to consider it. A commotion at the entrance caught his attention.

The short powerful figure of Jorge appeared from the boardwalk. Beside him was a slender sinuous form in black. Even before he felt the quick warning touch of Prudence's hand on his arm, Stark guessed the identity of the stranger.

"That's him!" she confirmed in a whisper. "The Konowa Kid."

The Kid and the gaucho had clearly just come off the trail. Mud clung to the tan duster the Kid wore over his black outfit, and Jorge was slapping dust off his hat. He stopped as his eyes fell on Stark. Sensing it, the Kid pulled up short as well.

Stark's first impulse to sneer contemptuously at the

young gunhawk faded as he noted the curious rig the Kid used to pack his iron, and the almost feminine delicacy of his movements.

Stark was used to gun-hungry punks looking to carve a notch in their reputation. Sometimes he felt as if he attracted them like a flame draws moths. A sign of his success in his violent trade, he'd grown to reckon.

But over the years he'd learned never to take their breed for granted. Someday he might make a slip, or be caught unawares, or finally run up against the man who was really faster than he was. Nope, it never paid to take for granted any hombre with a gun who had something to prove by using it on you.

But more than most of that kind, Stark decided, the Konowa Kid would bear watching.

Jorge said something in an aside to the Kid that made his gaze take on an odd intensity. He started to move forward, but Jorge laid a restraining hand on his arm. Arrogantly the Kid shrugged it off and advanced with mincing steps. Behind him, Jorge's flat mustached face betrayed disturbance and a little bit of confusion.

The Kid halted about six feet away. Stark wanted Prudence to move clear; she knew better than to hang this close. But for some reason she stuck near him.

"That fellow says you're the Peacemaker," the Kid declared belligerently. "I'm the Konowa Kid. Ever heard of me?"

"Nary a word," Stark said levelly.

"I figure that'll be changing," the Kid vowed. "See you have the little miss here with you."

Stark would've expected the Kid's eyes to shift, even briefly, to Prudence as he mentioned her. But the gunslick didn't make that greenhorn's mistake. His eyes, flat, colorless, remained fixed on Stark. Yeah, he'd bear watching all right.

Mentally Stark tried to catalogue the other men in the saloon. The confrontation between Prudence and Norene had weakened his usual alertness in some way. The hard cases Juan had been visiting with were still at their table. Jorge was edging up uncertainly behind the Kid.

"She's a mighty pretty little thing," the Kid voiced his appraisal of Prudence.

"Mighty," Stark agreed. "But not for the likes of you to talk about."

The Kid's hackles went up. "What are you saying?"

Stark's voice was icy. "I'm saying most yearlings who think they're fast with a gun end up wiggling their trigger finger once too often. Don't let that happen to you."

At last Prudence stepped to one side. She wasn't afraid, she just didn't want to get in his way if he had to act. Stark knew that was the only reason she had moved.

"You calling me a yearling?" the Kid flared.

"Nope. Just someone who thinks he's fast with a gun."

With a surprisingly light step Jorge moved between them, facing the Kid. One hand drifted down almost lazily to close on the Kid's fingers poised above his gun butt. Stark saw the young gunhawk's eyes go wide at what must be the strength in the gaucho's grip.

"*Bastante!* Enough!" Jorge muttered some other words Stark couldn't catch. He gestured toward the back of the saloon.

Slowly the fighting tension seeped out of the Kid's scrawny form. He jerked his hand free of Jorge's grip and turned sullenly away toward the tables. Jorge cast one last warning look over his shoulder at Stark, then cat-footed after the gunman.

"Come on." Stark caught Prudence's elbow. She didn't resist as he guided her to the door.

His right hand hovered close above his pistol. He kept his eyes roving over the occupants of the saloon, alert for

any yahoo who wanted to take up where the Konowa Kid
had been forced to leave off.

Outside he handed her up onto the wagon, then mounted
to the seat beside her and took the lines. Like a trained
scout, she twisted around to watch the front of the saloon,
the movement bringing her close against Stark.

"No one's following us," she said a little breathlessly
after a moment, and turned her face forward.

She still was close enough to him so that every bump of
the wagon jostled them together. Stark sensed that, under
the shared menace of the Konowa Kid's gun, the strife
between them had eased.

"What are the chances of the Kid making good on his
claim against the estate?" he queried.

"Not good at all," she asserted, "unless he can produce
more proof than I've yet seen or heard from him. If necessary, we can look for witnesses as to Jacob Langton's
whereabouts during the time in question, but I really doubt
it will come to that." She turned her head and gazed up at
Stark. "What do you make of him?"

"He belongs to Norene, I mean, the widow, just like you
figured. But she picked the wrong man, or boy, for the job.
He's a loose cannon. She's got Jorge riding herd on him
to keep him out of trouble. She doesn't want to risk him
getting himself killed."

Prudence shivered in recollection. "I don't care for that
foreman."

"Juan?"

"Yes." She shuddered again. "Don't ever leave me
alone with him."

"I tried to warn you," Stark pointed out.

She nodded soberly, then let a handful of seconds slip
by. When she spoke, her voice was hesitant. "What happened when you met with Mrs. Danner?"

Stark kept his eyes straight ahead. "I told you," he answered carelessly. "She tried to hire me. I turned her down."

"Is that all?" she probed softly.

Stark shifted on the hard seat. "I didn't tell you the price she offered to pay me." Irritation reared up suddenly in him. Where did she get off asking him questions like this? He snapped his head around to look down at her. "Pull in your claws, lady. Your eyes are starting to get as green as those of the widow woman."

She recoiled from him as though a whip had been popped in front of her face. "Are you implying I'm jealous?"

"Well," he drawled heavily, "you're doing a mighty good job of behaving like it."

"Do I have any reason to be?" she shot back.

"None that I know of!" Stark wasn't even sure what he meant by his words. Nor did he know if they were entirely true.

Prudence had no brand on him, and, even if she did, he hadn't yielded to the temptations of Norene's enticing charms. But, he had to admit, he had sure sought out those temptations. A man who did that, and expected not to succumb eventually, was a fool twice over.

They pulled up in front of the freight company in the gathering shadows of dusk. Stark kicked on the brake so hard it rocked the wagon. Prudence sat stiff and unyielding at his side. She made no effort to leave the vehicle.

"Now that you've had a chance to look things over, you can take the next stage back to South McAlister," Stark stated coldly.

"I'm not leaving."

"Why the blazes not?" Stark gritted.

"Don't talk that way to me!"

Stark tried to get a harness on his temper. "I thought

you'd see that it's dangerous for you here," he explained as reasonably as he could.

"It's dangerous for you too," she all but whispered. "For both of us."

"But it's what I'm paid for."

"Is it?"

Now Stark wasn't sure what *she* meant. "You think I can't handle the likes of the Konowa Kid?" he demanded to hide his bemusement.

"Oh, I'm sure you can outshoot and outfight whatever hard cases or bully boys beautiful Mrs. Norene Danner has on her payroll!"

"Well, then why in thunder won't you leave?" Stark stopped himself from saying anything further. He didn't know if he wanted her answer to that question, and he didn't know if she wanted to give it.

She waited in tense silence. When he failed to speak, she tossed her head. "I'll be going in now."

Before he could protest she stepped to the ground and headed toward the house.

Stark watched her go, then shook his head ruefully. He maneuvered the wagon under the shed, unhitched the mules, and turned them out to the corral.

He was returning the gear to the tack room when Clete's dry voice spoke from the gloom. "Don't throw down on me."

Stark berated himself mentally. He had to get that woman off his mind. A rogue bull buffalo could charge up on him, and he'd be none the wiser.

He lit the lantern and went about storing the tack, ignoring Clete's silent presence.

"Run into trouble at the Crimson Lady?" the aged teamster asked at last.

Stark snorted. "I ran into it before I ever left here."

"Miss McKay's a fine-looking lady," Clete commented.

"And more stubborn than any two mules we got in the string!"

"Yep." Clete nodded thoughtfully. "Just like somebody else I can think of."

"Some folks are too stubborn," Stark agreed. "Others talk too much."

"Only folks who mind a little talk are usually those hearing something they don't want to hear."

"Is that some old Pony Express rider proverb?"

"Happens one of them stubborn mules told me." Clete turned and shuffled off into the darkness.

Stark extinguished the lantern with an exasperated breath. He took a restless turn around the premises. He wasn't sure whether he was worried about Prudence or angry at her. He decided he was both.

Whispered voices made him draw up short. In the gloom beside the barn two figures who had been standing very close together moved quickly apart. Stark recognized Josh and Brenda.

"Hello, Mr. Stark," the boy said. He sounded out of breath. "We were just talking."

"Almost supper time, Brenda," Stark suggested.

"Yessir! I'll get it ready!" She hurried past him toward the house.

"I'll see to the mules!" Josh volunteered. He likewise disappeared.

Fool kids, Stark thought with what he was surprised to realize was a trace of envy.

Chapter Fifteen

The pistol-shot crack of a whip snapped Stark's head around sharply. He vaulted smoothly off the wagon seat as Brian brought the vehicle to a halt in front of the barn. They were just returning from a day-long run, and there was nothing about the freighting headquarters to suggest trouble in their absence. But that whipcrack hadn't sounded like the usual mule skinner's rawhide. It set off warning bells in Stark's mind.

He legged it through the length of the barn, then halted. He'd been right. The sound he'd heard had been that of a fighting whip. Clete's short wiry figure was in the corral. The mules had wisely retreated to the far side of the enclosure. Writhing a little with the movements of his arm, a good sixteen feet of tapered black leather lay in the dust in front of the ancient mule skinner.

As Stark caught sight of him, Clete's arm moved up over his head in the familiar circular motion of an expert whip man, and the serpent of leather disappeared. When his arm swept down out of the circle, the sharp pop sounded again.

"Not bad," Stark complimented. He recollected Clete's remark about having a fighting whip to match that of Juan. The old-timer hadn't been fooling. Stark waited until he was sure Clete was finished working the rawhide before he ambled closer.

"Got it out and oiled it today," Clete told him. "Figured it might come in handy. Here, try it." He passed the butt of the whip over.

Stark coiled it to get a feel for its heft. It was longer and heavier than a regular rawhide, and the weighted tip made it fly different than the poppers on the end of most bull-whips. The freshly oiled leather was sinuous and flexible in his hands. He fingered the pellet of lead sewed into the tip. A strike with such a piece would flay hide from man or beast alike.

Stark let the coils drop to the ground. He made the leather wriggle like a serpent in the dust. His first try was a lazy flex of his arm to get used to the weight and length. Then in a single continuous motion he whirled his arm overhead and threw it forward. He felt the released energy in the braided leather all the way down his arm as the weighted tip ripped the air with a crack of sound.

Clete nodded approval. He trotted into the barn, reappearing a moment later with a tin can which he set on a post. "Target practice." He grinned and moved clear.

Stark eyed the target as he approached to within range. He was out of practice. An expert with a whip like this could kill flies on a wall or extinguish a candle without touching the wick.

His arm moved in a blur. The whip cracked and the can skipped into the air. Stark stepped forward as fast as if he was throwing a punch, and struck again. Still in the air, the can danced as the lead tip dinged it once more.

Clete's eyes were wide. "Well, I'll be hanged!" he muttered.

Stark recoiled the rawhide and returned it to him. "Nice piece of leather," he commented, then added, "Things quiet while we were gone?"

"Not a peep out of the widow or her boys. Fellow that had been in her saloon stopped by to shoot the breeze. Said that the Konowa Kid was still blowing and going about taking you down, but Jorge wasn't letting him out of the bar. Juan didn't seem to be around, according to this fellow."

Stark pondered what Norene might have up her sleeve now. He reckoned there'd be some consequence or other to her meeting with him and Prudence the day before. He frowned. For now, it looked like they'd just have to wait for her next move.

"The girls will have supper ready shortly," Clete's voice brought him out of his broodings.

"Girls?" Stark echoed in puzzlement.

Clete's leathery face showed surprise. "Why, Brenda and Miss Prudence, of course."

Stark wagged his head. The notion of Prudence in the kitchen was a new one to him.

But she seemed to be as capable at that job as she was at taming a courtroom, Stark had to admit after the evening meal. Brenda gave Prudence full credit for the crisp golden fried chicken and the thick fluffy biscuits that accompanied it.

And Prudence herself looked to be in a lighthearted mood as she bustled about, deftly helping Brenda with the serving. She was fetching in a pretty yellow dress. But Stark could never quite catch her eye until the end of the meal when he bragged on her cooking.

She returned him an almost impersonal smile of thanks, and rose from the table to begin clearing the dishes.

Likely she was still rankled about the way they'd parted company the night before, he calculated with a tightening of his lips. But there didn't seem to be much he could do about it. She'd simmer down after a spell.

Shooed out of the house by the womenfolk, Stark and Clete were sipping coffee on the front porch when a gleaming buggy, pulled by a familiar steel-gray gelding, clattered into the yard. Carefully Stark set his cup aside.

"What in the Sam Hill . . . ?" Clete said sourly.

Stark glanced uneasily about, but no riders were following the buggy. Its driver was alone. The wan light from the vehicle's hanging lantern cast Norene Danner's features in a pale flattering glow.

"Truce?" she suggested with a smile as she brought the buggy to a halt in front of the porch. Noting their wariness, she tacked on, "I'm by myself. I don't need Juan with me whenever I go outdoors."

Stark rose to his feet. Norene was making her move. He just wasn't sure what it was. The door opened behind him, and he sensed Prudence's presence at his back.

"What do you want?" he asked Norene.

"Just to talk, Jim. Go for a ride with me?"

Stark hesitated, then started forward. He felt Prudence's hand clutch his arm.

"Jim, no." Her tone was a cross between a plea and a demand.

"I know what I'm doing," he said roughly and pulled free of her grip to descend the steps.

But did he? he questioned himself. Was he really hoping to learn something of use from this guileful seductress, or was he flirting once more with temptation in order to defy Prudence, or to prove something to himself?

Norene scooted over for him to clamber in beside her

under the canopy. There was barely enough room for them both. Perforce, he was pressed close, and felt her lean gently against him. She didn't offer to give him the lines, but jigged the horse forward almost immediately.

Beneath a dark cape she wore a red dress, and the lantern spread a crimson glow from it across her neckline. The thick mane of her hair hung free and shimmering. She put her head back and laughed with pleasure as they left the yard.

Stark eyed her curiously.

"Just like going out with a beau when I was a girl," she answered his unasked question. "I haven't felt like this in years."

Stark didn't answer. Had she ever been as young and innocent as she sounded?

She guided the conveyance off the main road and onto a narrow track that wound deeper into the cottonwoods and willows. The night air was cool, but Stark found he was sweating. The shroud of branches overhead obscured the early stars, and he had a sensation of being trapped.

She stopped in a secluded glen, maneuvering the horse with practiced ease. Plainly she had used this spot before, for what purposes Stark didn't want to guess.

The trees were a black wall around them. Stark disliked the lantern. It made the buggy too easy a target. But he figured he was close enough to her to discourage any bushwhacker that might be lurking in ambush.

She put on the brake and tied off the reins. The gelding snorted, then stood quiet. A faint breeze whispered through the bare branches like the voice of an errant spirit.

Norene twisted about toward him. "We need to talk, Jim."

"I'm listening."

She lifted a pale hand as though to brush his cheek with

her palm. He caught her wrist and pushed it firmly down. "You said you wanted to talk."

"Don't be that way, Jim," she implored softly.

He released her hand. She left it where it was, barely touching the side of his leg. "I'm still listening."

Her sigh was bewitching. "We should've met a long time ago, when we were both younger. Maybe things could've been different; maybe I could've been different."

"We both made our own choices all the way down the line. That's why we're not alike. We took different trails."

"Did we? They both brought us here."

"I didn't choose your trail, lady."

"All right," she conceded. "We've both lived by our choices. I'm not proud of everything I've done, but I don't regret my choices. And I'll make one now. I'll choose you over that two-bit freight line."

"Meaning what?"

"Your little lady lawyer can have the B&B. I'll call off my dogs."

"In return for what?"

"You," she whispered. "Throw in with me like I offered before. I need a man like you. I'll send Juan and his brother packing. Juan's a top-notch ramrod, but he can't think for himself. He doesn't have your brains. His brother's nothing but a wolf on a leash."

"Juan might have something to say about those plans."

She uttered a wordless sound of exasperation. "He won't defy me, and if he does, you can take care of him. You're a fighting man too. My other men will back you if I give the order. They've got no love for Juan."

Neither did she, apparently. Her loyalties shifted like the prairie winds.

"This won't even have to interfere with you and that prim and proper lady lawyer. Once the estate is settled, she'll be back in Guthrie. If you want to go pay her a visit every so often, what do I care? I like to have some fun on the side too. None of that would matter between us, so long as we understand each other.''

''Prudence doesn't have any ties on me,'' Stark denied.

Her chuckle was low and throaty and skeptical. ''So much the better then.'' Her voice took on a breathless urgency, ''Think about it, Jim. You could have everything you've ever wanted. Wealth, power. Me.''

What did he want? Stark thought. Her hand slid up over his leg. She leaned even closer, pressing herself against him, burying her face in his shoulder. Her hair caressed his jaw. Her alluring scent was in his nostrils. The blood pounded in his head.

But Stark's mind shifted to a lovely face, dusky hair, and dark eyes that could flash like prairie lightning. He pictured a trim petite figure, and fancied he felt the light touch of a gently restraining hand on his chest.

In the end, it didn't take much effort at all to close his hands on Norene's shoulders and push her firmly back from him. She stared at him with a hurt mystified expression that he could almost, but not quite, believe was genuine.

''It's not in the cards, sister,'' he said.

''What do you mean?''

''I wouldn't work for you, or throw in with you, on a dare. I'd end up in harness with a bit in my teeth, and you in the driver's seat working the reins and plying the whip.''

She stiffened beneath his hands, but there wasn't the explosion of rage he had expected. Quickly she turned her head aside so the burnished copper veil of her hair hid her expression.

''You're wrong, Jim. It wouldn't be like that.'' Her words were muffled. ''If you'd let me try, I could convince you.''

''I'm already convinced,'' Stark told her coldly. ''Four

men trying to kill me and a teenage kid in a blizzard convinced me real fast.''

She shook her head, still not looking at him. ''That wasn't my doing, Jim. It was Juan. He did all that without my knowledge or my approval. Can't you believe that?'' At last she lifted her face to him. He was amazed to see the reflection of tears on her face.

He let go of her. ''It's no good, Norene. Even if I did believe you, there's too much water under the bridge now.'' He kept his tone impersonal, but for a moment, in spite of himself, he mused over what it would've been like if he really had met her when they were both young. He reckoned he knew the answer. She'd chosen her trail a long time ago. It was a dark and crooked one, and led nowhere he wanted to go.

''I'm sorry you feel that way, Jim. I can't say it doesn't hurt me plenty. But I'll still back off from the B&B. I'll leave you and the kids alone.''

Schemes piled on top of schemes, Stark reflected darkly. ''Good enough,'' he said aloud, and reached past her to untie the reins.

She didn't speak as he drove them back to the freight company. When he passed the lines to her she took them without protest, her hands brushing his.

''Good night, Jim.''

''Vaya con Dios,'' he said softly, ''Go with God.'' He didn't figure she'd take the advice.

He stood and watched as the vehicle clattered away into the gloom. The light of her lantern was swallowed up by darkness.

Clete stepped out of the shadows. ''No wounds, anyway,'' he commented dryly.

''None that show,'' Stark was terse. ''Get everybody together. We need to have a confab.''

"I'll fetch Josh to spell me as lookout." Clete swung away.

They gathered in the kitchen. Once more Stark leaned against the wall. The Langton kids and Clete waited for him to speak. He couldn't read the strange set expression of Prudence's face, or the dark intensity of her eyes.

"The widow's not going to give up," he stated flatly. "She's got her loop spread for this outfit, and she's not going to stop until it's under her brand."

"So what do we do?" Brian burst out angrily. "Just sit here and wait for her to come at us again?"

Stark shook his head. No. We take the fight to her."

Brian's eyes lit up. Prudence tensed, her shoulders squaring.

"We're fools if we play her game any longer," Stark went on. "Eventually she'll wear us down or one of her gunhands will get lucky. If we stay on the defensive, she'll win."

Norene's repentant promises still echoed softly in his ears. Just like her, they were a deceit, a sleight of hand trick to fool rubes. He was no rube, and he was fed up to his neck with letting her be in the driver's seat. Time for him to take the reins himself.

"What have you got in mind?" Clete drawled.

"James, I won't have you provoking violence or deliberately setting out to settle things with your gun!" Prudence snapped before Stark could answer. Her spine was as rigid as that of the straightback chair in which she sat.

"The violence has already been provoked. And how do you figure I've been settling things up until now?"

"I wouldn't know what dubious methods you've chosen to use!" Her eyes blazed. "But I will not permit you to engage in some puerile display of violence that will, no doubt, place your own life at risk, as well as those of all of us here. Remember, you work for me!"

"That's right," Stark countered. "You hired me as your troubleshooter and put me in charge of that. It's too late to back out, and now I aim to do my job!" Wheeling, he strode from the room and out of the house.

Chapter Sixteen

The Crimson Lady was crowded with early evening rev-
elers, Stark saw as he entered. In addition to a scattering
of Norene's hired guns, there were cowpunchers, a few
farmers, some townsfolk, and a couple of drummers. A
haze of cigarette smoke stung his eyes, and the odor of
alcohol seared his nostrils. The roulette wheel clattered, and
voices murmured. Good, there would be plenty of
witnesses.

Juan was nowhere to be seen, nor was Norene. But Jorge
was by himself at a corner table near the end of the bar,
where his charge, the Konowa Kid, was treating a bored-
looking floozy to some raw whiskey and loud boasting.

Stark smiled thinly and moved forward. His entry caused
a quietening of the talk for a moment. He ignored it. Jorge's
chair scraped as he pushed it back. The Konowa Kid looked
around at last and spotted Stark over the bar girl's bare
shoulder. Wordlessly the Kid shoved her aside. Her out-

raged complaint broke off sharply as she turned and saw Stark's looming figure. Hastily she drew away.

"What are you doing here?" the Kid snarled. The whiskey didn't look to have dulled his alertness.

"Thought I'd have a drink," Stark answered casually.

His senses were on a hair trigger, but he didn't think Norene's boys would interfere if there was trouble between him and the Kid, especially seeing as how the Kid had been mouthing challenges ever since he'd hit town.

"You ain't drinking in any bar where I am!"

As expected, the Kid was making this easy. "Guess you better shake a leg then," Stark told him coldly.

The saloon had gone quiet. Even the roulette wheel rattled to a halt. The Kid's feminine face darkened and turned ugly with feral violence. "You telling me to leave?" he blustered.

Stark shrugged. "Your choice, but I'm having a drink."

"The devil you are!" The Kid faced him full on, hand poised near his slantwise gun.

There were a couple of yards between them, and Stark wasn't surprised when Jorge's sturdy bulk slid easily into the space. His eyes met Stark's. "You not fight him," he announced in his heavy English.

"You figuring to take his place?"

"This is my fight!" the Kid objected loudly from behind Jorge's broad shoulders.

"Wait your turn, sonny," Stark advised. He had calculated this was coming. Better to get Jorge out of the way first.

If he could.

He nodded at Jorge's holster. "You're packing iron. Go ahead and make your play."

Jorge shook his head slowly back and forth. "I no fight you with *pistolas*." His lips peeled back from square yellow mule's teeth. "You good with feet. I fight that way too." He shuffled his steel-toed boots in his little dance step. "These my weapons."

Somewhere in the room a man uttered an excited oath.

Jorge drifted away from the bar. He was up on his toes with his hands in front of his chest, fingertips just touching. Yep, this was *capoeira* all right.

Stark tried to marshal what he knew of the pagan fighting art. Developed by black slaves in Brazil in order to defend themselves against their owners, *capoeira* owed many of its movements to the old tribal dances of the slaves' African homelands. Since their hands were often chained, they had to rely mostly on their feet for fighting. Teaching the art was now officially banned in Brazil, but the practice of it still thrived.

The saloon's patrons had cleared an area in front of the bar. Stark raised his fists up like a prizefighter, and decided not to wait for the gaucho to trot out any of his fancy tricks. With no crouch or flexing of legs to signal his intent, Stark sprang forward, twisting his lead left foot out sidewards. Jorge didn't have time to block or move out of the way. He grunted as Stark's boot rammed his midriff.

The impact barely fazed him. Instantly he dived forward onto his hands and spun his whole body on them as a pivot. His legs swept around in an arc that caught Stark's ankles like a rolling log. Stark hit the barroom floor on his side. Completing his spin, Jorge was just whirling past him. Stark cocked a leg and lashed out. Jorge grunted as he was knocked rolling. He bounced back onto his feet.

As Stark came erect, the gaucho tucked his head and dived into a forward somersault. He stiffened his legs as he completed the roll, both boots catching Stark in the gut before he could pull clear. Winded, Stark was driven stumbling back toward the wall. Customers scrambled from his path just before he fetched up hard against it. He had a gasping moment to realize he'd never run across anything quite like *capoeira,* and that, using it, Jorge's steel-toed boots could kill him just as surely as a bullet from the Konowa Kid's gun.

Jorge cartwheeled forward, literally standing on his hands like a circus acrobat. His flailing boots lashed at Stark's head where he stood pinned against the wall. Stark ducked aside. Jorge's boots met the wall hard enough to shake the building. Stark kicked out and missed as Jorge somersaulted clear. He might never get a chance to match guns with the Kid if he couldn't get past this human windmill.

Stark went after him, kicking, using first one foot, then the other. He swung a stiffened leg across in an arc at Jorge's head, swept it back without it ever touching down. Jorge bobbed away, then swayed like a snake to evade the snapping front kick and the roundhouse which followed. He sidestepped to let Stark's final plunging thrust kick go past him to splinter the front of the bar.

Stark recoiled and caught his balance to find Jorge facing him, leaning forward a little, arms spread. His stance gave Stark a glimmer of what was coming next. He was already bending low when Jorge whirled on the axis of his hips, his spinning body actually suspended parallel to the floor. His boots came around like twin scythes and swept over Stark's lowered head. With no target to hit, Juan kicked off from the bar in midair and landed in the same leaning position, arms curved in front of him.

He made Stark think of a giant human spider, and from that, Stark's mind kicked into a gallop. A spider was all legs, and so far this fight had been carried on using nothing but legs and feet. Jorge's extended head made a tempting target for another kick, and he could be expecting it. But *savate* included European-style pugilism as well as foot techniques, and in this duel of foot fighters, the gaucho might not be expecting naked fists.

Stark feinted a kick at his offered head. Jorge reared back a bit, and Stark blurred in, his fists slashing. He caught Jorge with a savage left-right combination that snapped his head back and forth. Stark pressed him. His clenched hands flashed, winging in punches from all sides and all angles. Finally an uppercut with Stark's shoulder under it drove Jorge clear of the final hooking left.

Jorge dived to one side. His right hand met the floor, and he pivoted on that arm, swinging the steel toe of his boot around at Stark's knee. Stark skipped aside and booted him rolling with a swiping swing of his leg.

Stark was almost on top of him as Jorge let the roll propel him to his feet. He lashed out high at Stark's head. throwing his shoulders back and flinging his arms down behind him to catch himself. Stark saw the gleaming metal toe of the tooled boot driving at his face. He shot his hands up, caught Jorge's ankle, and twisted like he was bulldogging a steer. Jorge tumbled with the motion. His booted foot was torn from Stark's grasp.

But the wrenched leg buckled as he regained his feet, and for the first time, pain writhed across his broad face. He stretched his arms wide, standing on one leg as if he was doing a ballet. He twirled at Stark. The foot of his injured leg—still dangerous—hooked at Stark's skull.

Stark squatted low and kicked like a Russian dancer, snapping his leg straight out. The hard toe of his boot tore into the knee of Jorge's anchor leg. Bone snapped. Jorge bellowed in agony and crashed down, legs flailing. Stark moved in, bent and reached to snatch the fallen man's gun from its holster. He flung it away. Jorge was out of the fight; he wouldn't be doing any more fancy footwork for a good long spell.

Stark swiveled up onto his feet to face the Konowa Kid.

The Kid was standing clear of the bar. His pretty face was alight with some dark passion. The pearl handle of his pistol shone starkly against the black of his garb. His hand hovered near it like some evil insect.

"I'm still hankering for that drink," Stark drawled.

Other than Jorge's grunting moans, the saloon had gone dead quiet. Stark's hands were aching from the battering he had given Jorge, but not badly enough, he hoped, to interfere with his draw. No one was looking to butt in, he understood. Private showdown.

The Kid's Adam's apple bobbed in his skinny neck. "You—" he spat furiously, and finished whatever he was saying by going for his gun. His hand darted for the pearl-handled pistol slung across his midriff.

Stark pulled and fired with the speed of a cracking whip. The Kid's gun was clear of leather and swinging toward him when Stark's heavy .45 slug drilled his scrawny shoulder and slammed him back off his feet. Shrouded in smoke, Stark paced forward and stood over the fallen man where he slumped against the bar.

"I warned you about wiggling your trigger finger," Stark told him. "You should've listened."

The Kid was clutching at his wounded shoulder. "I need a doctor!" he gasped.

Stark cocked the .45 and pointed it straight down at the Kid's wide-eyed face. "I'll doctor you with a bullet if you don't answer my questions."

The Kid gawked up at him. "Huh? What?"

"You heard me." Stark's tone was remorseless. "You'll get a sawbones if you talk. Who do you ride for? Who hired you to come here pretending to be Jacob Langton's son?"

Stark sensed a stirring among the spectators as his words penetrated the room. He was most aware of the watching hard cases. They had just seen him run roughshod over two fighting men, each on his own terms. Lacking direct orders, they weren't anxious to tangle with him. Nor had they figured it was any of their business to take sides in a private feud. But now that their employer's interests could be at risk, they might see things a mite different.

"Hold on there," one of them blustered, half rising from his seat.

"Let the man ask his questions a gravel-toned voice cut off the protest.

The wiry figure of Clete Hatfield moved into view at the edge of Stark's vision. The massive Beaumont-Adams revolver looked too big for his knobby fist, but it held dead steady on the tableful of hard cases. With a disgruntled look on his swarthy face, the jasper who had spoken sank back into his chair.

"Figured you might need someone to cover your back," Clete addressed Stark without taking his eyes off the gunsharps.

"Glad to have you along."

"Now you boys just sit tight and let these two fellows carry on with their palavering," Clete continued reasonably. "There might be some things said that folks here would have an interest in. Might even be of concern to you."

Stark waggled the .45 back and forth a little. The Kid's colorless eyes were crossed from trying to look down the barrel. "Talk," Stark prompted coldly.

"You'll get me a doc if I tell you?"

"You won't need one if you don't speak up pretty quick." It was a lie, but the Kid didn't have to know that.

"What do you want? For heaven's sakes, I'll tell you!"

"Who hired you?"

Sweat gleamed on the Kid's face. "The widow woman! Mrs. Danner," he managed.

"She told you to claim to be Jacob Langton's son?"

"That's right!"

Stark heard some of the locals mutter at this revelation. "What's your real name?"

"Otis Beedler."

"Well, Otis, have you worked for Mrs. Danner before?"

"Yeah, sure. Whenever she needed something special, she knew how to get hold of me."

"Did you kill Jacob Langton?"

"What? No! Are you crazy?" the Kid babbled. "I never—"

"What about Old Man Danner? Did you kill him?"

"Accidents! They was both accidents! Ask anybody!"

"I'm asking you. And I won't put up with another lie."

"I didn't do it! Honest!"

"Who did?"

The Kid's eyes darted frantically but kept coming back to the ominous hole of the .45's barrel. "I don't know for sure, but word is among her hands that the big hombre, Juan, did both of them on the widow's orders." He bit down hard as though to cut off further words.

But he'd already said plenty. There was a rising chorus of whispers and low voices among the townsfolk and cowboys. The two drummers had been getting an earful as well. The hired guns were grim and watchful.

"On your feet," Stark ordered the Kid. "I'll get you patched up."

"On my feet? I can't get up!"

Impatiently Stark reached down, caught his good arm and yanked him upright. The Kid's limb felt like a pipecleaner in his fist. "You can stand, and you can walk. Come on!"

Half supporting and half dragging his slumping form, Stark backed toward the door, the Colt still in his hand. He saw Jorge had passed out on the floor. Both legs were bent at awkward angles.

"Go on, get the Kid out of here," Clete directed. "I'll cover you."

Stark holstered his gun and steered his charge out the door. A moment later Clete backed out of the saloon and joined him. "You folks just keep your seats!" he called back into the bar.

No one seemed disposed to challenge his instructions.

"What now?" he demanded.

Stark had only a rough plan. He hadn't been sure he'd make it this far. "We need to get him to the sawbones, then put him on ice—maybe in the jail—until I can get some law down here from McAlister. What he said in front of witnesses in there is enough to get the U.S. marshal's office interested. I'll ride there tonight. If I push, I can be back tomorrow. It ain't safe to send a telegram. Norene would learn what I'm planning."

Clete nodded. "All right. No use putting him in the hoosegow here. Our local lawdog would sit up and beg when Juan came looking."

"You got a better idea?"

"So happens I know an old drifter's shack where I can store him until morning. Nobody's likely to stumble on him there."

"That should give me all the time I need. I'll bring Chris Madsen back with me. He's working out of McAlister." The Kid had become a limp weight in Stark's arms. "He's fainted. What about his wounds?"

"Forget Doc Harrison. I doubt he can be trusted." Clete seemed to be enjoying himself. "I can patch this sorry pup up myself good enough to last till you get back." He gave his grizzled head a shake. "By Godfrey, I wish I was making that ride instead of you. Reminds me of the old days in the Express."

Stark knew his plan was a gamble. But riding Red, he calculated, he could get to McAlister and return with the redoubtable Chris Madsen before Norene could sort out what had happened, come up with any sort of workable strategy, and put it into play.

"Where's this shack?" he queried. "We better get him to it pronto."

"Never mind helping me pack him there," Clete said. "He ain't much of a load. I'll toss him over my mule. You best hit the trail."

Stark didn't argue. He waited long enough to see Clete on his way, then stepped up into the saddle and reined Red about. The big sorrel snorted, sensing his tension.

"We got us a ride to make, boy," Stark told him.

He put the stallion through the cottonwoods and out onto the vast expanse of prairie. The grasslands glowed silver under the moonlit night sky. Red stretched out into a run, and, with a silent prayer on his lips, Stark settled himself into the rhythm of the ride.

Chapter Seventeen

"Clete, I don't like this at all," Prudence stated.

Clete leaned back in his chair at the kitchen table. He sipped his morning coffee and grinned. "Now, Miss Prudence, there's no cause for getting upset. All we did, or, rather, Jim did, was apprehend a confessed criminal. Now we're holding him for the proper authorities. We're just being good upstanding citizens."

Prudence frowned. "We've got a wounded man tied up in a shack," she pointed out as sternly as she could manage. "To get him there, you and Jim committed assault and battery, kidnapping, and false imprisonment."

"That's right, Miss Prudence," Clete agreed with a twinkle in his eye. "Ain't that what I just said?"

Prudence shook her head helplessly. "You missed your calling, Clete. You should've been a lawyer."

Clete put on a mock scowl. "Coming from a man, them'd be fighting words!"

Prudence had to laugh. But she was fully aware that this

was nothing to laugh about. And she was just as aware that, in a real sense, Clete was right.

Further, she grudgingly conceded, Jim Stark had been right also, after a fashion. His precipitous actions, violent though they had been, had given them, in the person of the Konowa Kid and his coerced public confession, the tools that could be used to put an end to Norene Danner's illegal persecution of the B&B. She prayed Stark would get back soon.

Her thoughts and emotions, as usual, seemed all in a tumble when it came to him. Anger and humiliation, affection and worry, all chased each other about within her. His open defiance of her in front of others still smarted. But, knowing Jim, could she really have expected anything different from him?

A secret part of her persisted in feeling pride that he had overcome two professional hard cases in violent confrontations. And, she reminded herself, he hadn't killed anyone in the process. For that, at least, she could be grateful.

And where was he now? He should be well on his way back to Doaksville with the deputy marshal to quash the trouble here. She imagined him riding hard across the prairie on his big sorrel, the wind in his handsome face, his jaw set in firm determination.

Could this jumble of emotions in her breast be love?

She didn't know where *that* notion had come from, and she recoiled sharply, banishing it with such quickness that she could almost pretend it had never entered her mind.

By personality and profession she was a thinking, logical individual who believed in facing life and making decisions based on rational mental processes. To have such thoughts and emotions about him was embarrassing. Logically, rationally, she knew she could not be in love with him. He was too . . . too violent and arrogant.

And yet, she acknowledged, he had been correct when

he accused her of acting like a jealous woman. How could she be jealous over a man in whom she had no romantic interest? It must be that she hated the idea of a good man like Jim Stark being preyed upon by a brazen harlot like Norene Danner. The nerve of the woman! Intellectually she knew Stark had not yielded to her decadent charms. But the cavalier manner in which he had gone off with her in the buggy, almost at the snap of her fingers, and over her own objections, still rankled.

"He'll be all right. He's no greenhorn; he can handle pretty much anything that comes down the pike," Clete's voice intruded.

"Who do you mean?" Prudence asked with as much innocent perplexity as she could summon. She could feel warmth rising to her face.

Clete snorted. "Don't try kidding an old kidder, gal!"

From outside the house came the sudden raucous barking of the dogs. Hoofbeats pounded, and a pair of shots rang out. Alarm flashed across Clete's lined face. He surged out of his chair with the speed of a much younger man, and bolted from the kitchen toward the parlor, pulling his pistol as he went. A moment later came a gun blast that seemed to vibrate the walls of the house. Clete chortled in triumph, but the dogs were still barking.

On her feet, Prudence hesitated. She needed a gun if she was to be of any help, and, foolishly, she had not deigned to wear one. As she paused, Brenda burst into the kitchen from the rear of the house where she'd been cleaning. Her blue eyes were wide, but she carried a revolver competently enough in one slim brown hand.

"What is it?" she cried. "What's happening?"

The sound of wood splintering came from the front door. Clete roared with rage. Gunfire boomed and thundered. Clete came reeling back into the kitchen. Prudence saw with horror that the side of his head was bloody. His left arm hung limp and bloodstained. He crashed to the floor almost at her feet and didn't move again.

Brenda screamed, high and shrill like an Indian brave. She thrust her pistol forward and fired. The bullet scarred the wood of the doorjamb just as a massive male figure, poncho swirling about him, barrelled low into the room. His shoulder brushed Prudence aside in passing, then he closed in on Brenda. His big hand twisted her arm effortlessly aside, and the revolver clattered to the floor. She kicked at his booted shins, and he swung the open palm of his other hand in a resounding slap that sent the teenage girl flying senseless into the corner.

Prudence lunged for the rack of butcher knives on the counter. Her fingers gripped the hilt of one, and she whirled, thrusting straight out with it exactly as Stark had told her to do, in some past time of shared danger.

Her proper technique was of no avail. The gleaming blade snagged in the heavy fabric of the billowing poncho. Then the same hand that had so easily disarmed Brenda clamped on her wrist with such massive crushing pressure that her fingers opened involuntarily to let the knife fall.

Juan laughed and hugged her tight against him with immense lecherous enjoyment. Her face was buried in the wool of his poncho. She smelled his foul sweat in it, tasted the bitter salt in her mouth. She was helpless as a child against his brutal dominating strength.

"Let her go! You don't touch her unless I say so!"

Prucence felt the powerful arms reluctantly loosen. She twisted furiously free, catching a glimpse of the brooding scowl that darkened Juan's dissolute features. Wheeling, Prudence faced her rescuer.

Norene Danner looked both gorgeous and evil. Clad in a black riding outfit trimmed in red, she had her scarlet hair drawn severely back. Her green eyes were flashing with a rage that, for the moment, was directed at her paramour. Two hard-faced gunmen bulked in the doorway behind her.

Prudence understood dismally that her reprieve might be only temporary.

"Do you hear me?" Norene blazed furiously at Juan. "I won't have you handling her without my say-so! She's nothing but a scrawny, little, fancy-talking trollop anyway! Now get out there and look for Stark!"

Juan's lip curled like a dog preparing to snarl, but he shoved past the two gunmen who readily yielded to him. Prudence heard him slam out of the house.

Her mind was reeling, but she fought to compose herself as Norene confronted her. The taller woman's blouse heaved with the strength of her emotions.

"You can't possibly believe you can get away with this!" Prudence exclaimed.

"Oh, I can get away with it, honey. Just you keep watching!" Norene pressed close, towering over her. Prudence refused to give ground.

"Where are they? Where's Stark and that weasely little backstabbing gunfighter?"

Prudence had only a second to debate her answer. If Norene learned Stark was returning from McAlister in the company of a U.S. deputy, she'd have her men laying in wait for them. The best policy was to keep her uncertain.

"I have no idea where they are," she replied with cold defiance.

For a moment she thought Norene would strike her, but then the redhead seized control of herself. Faintly from outside came a curious rhythmic popping sound.

Norene turned to the closest gunman and gestured at Brenda's sprawled form. "Get her up. Make sure she's all right. I hope that big ox didn't hurt her. We need her and the boy alive."

Brenda had started to stir, Prudence saw with relief. The

girl moaned and shook her head, her hair in disarray, as the hard case hauled her to her feet.

"Take her outside," Norene ordered.

Brenda's pretty face was just beginning to show shocked comprehension as she was hustled out. Prudence looked desperately around for the knife or a discarded gun—anything that could serve as a weapon. But there was no way she could hope to physically oppose their captors now.

"Take her too."

A hard hand gripped Prudence's arm. None of them had paid any heed to Clete's crumpled shape. He looked small and frail. Prudence could see no sign of life in him. Her heart sinking, she let herself be escorted roughly out the door.

As they emerged from the house she faltered. Juan was just recoiling a huge black whip. A prone figure lay nearby in the dust, shirt in tatters, back lacerated. Prudence saw it was Josh. She remembered the popping sound she'd heard, and shuddered. In his rage Juan had laid his whip to the boy.

Norene took in the tableau as well. "You sadistic beast!" she snapped at the gaucho.

She evidenced no concern over his victim's welfare. She was only using the incident as a chance to once more vent her spleen on her ramrod. Juan fingered his whip and stared after her as she stalked past him.

"Your Peacemaker is not here!" he called jeeringly at her retreating back.

There were all kinds of emotions twisting and writhing between that pair, Prudence thought dazedly.

She found herself, along with Brenda, being taken none too gently to where a pair of men were assembling the raiders' horses. Brenda was crying silently from the sight of Josh. Prudence wished helplessly that she could somehow comfort her.

She wasn't sure of the exact method, but it was obvious that the lightning assault—no doubt led by Juan—had overwhelmed the B&B's weakened defenses. There had been at least one casualty among the attackers. She saw a dead man already slung over an uneasy horse. She remembered poor Clete's cackle of triumph.

"No sign of the Kid," a shifty-eyed character reported to Norene.

The widow was mostly over her blazing fury. "Never mind. We'll learn his whereabouts soon enough. Get the boy. Let's move out."

Brian was brought from the barn. He had an angry bruise showing on his forehead under his touseled tow hair. Two men held his arms, despite the fact his hands were tied behind his back. He glared about, but looked relieved upon spotting Prudence and Brenda. He wasn't wasting his breath on futile protestations.

Quickly Prudence and Brenda were likewise bound. Then the trio of captives were heaved astride spare horses. Prudence was remotely grateful for the divided riding skirt she wore.

"Shall we burn this place?" Juan asked, with an ugly yearning, from the saddle of his palomino.

"No," Norene answered curtly. "It would take too long. Anyway, we'll have use for it eventually."

Her words didn't bode well for their futures, Prudence mused bleakly. But there had been little reason for hope ever since Juan had exploded through the kitchen doorway. She could only pray that Stark would arrive soon, although what even he could achieve against such odds was questionable. He and the deputy might only be riding to their deaths.

Her mind was numb from a growing sense of shock that spread through her like a cold tide. She paid little heed to the route their captors took. There was no way to communicate with her fellow prisoners.

She forced herself to some degree of alertness as they at length mounted a grassy bluff that dropped steeply away to the tree-lined course of a stream. Before them, built in a rough U shape, were the decaying limestone ruins of more than a dozen buildings of varying sizes, none over two stories in height. A single sagging log structure remained at the bottom of the U next to the creek.

Norene led her small command straight up the center of the compound. Prudence saw scattered junk in the tall grass—broken jugs and glassware, splintered wagon wheels, even the rusting barrel of a cannon. They passed a couple of old foundations. She realized this must be all that was left of legendary Fort Towson.

Once a bulwark of the Army's power on the expanding Western frontier, the fort had long since been abandoned and left to the depredations of human scavengers. They had carted off most of the salvageable material for use in the construction of towns like Doaksville and local homes. None of the remaining shells of buildings had roofs left on them. The limestone gleamed white and skeletal in the bright heatless sunshine. The square frames of windows gaped forlornly.

They were riding straight up what must've once been the parade ground. Soldiers and their families, many of them long dead now, had once drilled, lived, and perhaps fought here on these premises. Prudence hoped she and her companions weren't going to be added to the ranks of ghosts manning this decaying outpost.

They dismounted in front of the single remaining log structure. Whatever purpose it had once served, it was now in sorry shape. But as a hideout for the kidnappers, it seemed ideal.

The three captives were herded into the main room of

the structure by Norene, Juan and two other gunhawks. "Cut them loose," the redhead commanded.

Juan pulled a wicked knife that reminded Prudence of Stark's bowie, and cut the leather thongs binding them. Prudence rubbed her wrists thankfully. Brian looked as though he wanted to fight, but knew better than to try against the odds confronting them.

"Sit down," Norene indicated a rickety table.

When they were seated she produced a sheaf of papers and put them on the table with a fountain pen. "Sign these, all of you."

Prudence slid the papers toward her and scanned them. "These won't stand up in court," she announced, lifting her head to meet Norene's gaze.

"I don't need your opinion, Little Miss Lawyer. I don't know much about the law, but I do know that assignments executed by all three of you conveying the B&B to me, lock, stock and barrel, will carry some weight in a court."

She was right, Prudence admitted to herself, provided the three of them weren't alive to testify to the contrary.

"We won't sign!" Brian declared hotly.

"Oh, you'll sign, sonny. Or maybe you'd like for me to have Juan do a little romancing with the lady lawyer. Or better yet, with your sweet young sister here."

Brian surged halfway to his feet before Juan's big hand clamped on his shoulder from behind and slammed him back into his seat. The gaucho's ravaged face was set in a lecherous grin of evil anticipation.

"Why are you doing this?" Prudence fought to keep her voice level. "The B&B can't be worth this much to you."

"Maybe it wasn't at one time," Norene acknowledged coldly. "But it is now. And I'll own it."

"You'll have to get past James Stark before you do!" Brenda flared up suddenly.

Norene's red lips twisted savagely. "Stark's a fool and

a weakling. He can't beat me. Any man who'd turn down what I offered—'' She broke off abruptly as she saw the triumphant smile of understanding that came unbidden to Prudence's face.

"It's about him now, isn't it?" Prudence demanded with supreme assurance. "You didn't like being spurned. Well, listen to me, lady. You don't have Jim, and you never will."

Norene reached her in a single swift stride. Prudence saw the slap coming, but couldn't duck away quite fast enough. Her ears rang, and she had to catch herself to keep from being knocked out of her chair. But when she raised her head, she still wore a mocking trace of her smile.

Norene whirled on Juan. "Get outside. Keep watch for Stark. I don't put it past him to track us here somehow."

Juan nodded and moved toward the door with a catlike tread that had an awful, pent up eagerness to it. "If he comes, we'll be waiting for him," he promised grimly, and then he was gone.

Chapter Eighteen

Stark felt his hackles rise in instinctive warning as he rode up to the B&B. The scent of trouble was in the air. Red was almost sagging beneath him. He'd put the sorrel through a hard ride to McAlister and back.

And it had all been for nothing.

The exhaustion that had weighed upon him more heavily over the past hours slipped away in a heartbeat. He palmed the Colt as he ran his searching gaze over the seemingly deserted freight headquarters.

A figure stirred in the shadows of the porch, and Stark lined the Colt.

"Go easy," Clete's weary voice said. "They're gone now."

He emerged into view, and Stark saw he had his left arm in a sling. A fresh ugly wound creased the side of his grizzled skull, like a straight branding iron had been laid there.

"Who's gone?" Stark rasped as he slid from the sorrel.

166

"What happened?" But he could already guess the answers.

"The widow woman and her boys hit us this morning," Clete confirmed his fears. "Best I can figure, Juan made like an Indian and sneaked in close enough to lay Josh out before he could give a warning. He's in bad shape. They shot me up and left me for dead."

Stark swallowed hard and clamped down on the unfamiliar panic rising up within him. "What about Prudence? And the kids?"

"They took them," Clete answered flatly. "When I came to, I got Doc Harrison to patch up me and Josh. Then I set out to track them. They're holed up in what's left of the old trading post at Fort Towson. I reckon Miss Prudence and the kids are still alive. Once I had them located, I came back here, figuring you'd be showing up soon." He gave his head a slow rueful shake. "Couldn't do nothing else. I wasn't in any kind of shape to try taking them by my lonesome."

"I'm in some kind of shape to do it," Stark said tersely.

"Figure I can side you, leastways." Clete frowned. "Where's the deputy marshal?"

"Off on the trail of a couple of owlhoots who robbed a stage," Stark advised bleakly. "I left word for him to head down here pronto when he gets back. There wasn't anybody else around to lend us a hand, so I hightailed it back."

There was no time for blaming himself for drawing the lightning down on the B&B, Stark knew. It would've struck anyway, sooner or later. But Prudence's soft voice and her words about Juan echoed hauntingly in his ears. "Don't ever leave me alone with him," she'd said.

And here he'd gone and done just that.

"Where's Josh?" he asked aloud. "Can he fight?"

Clete jerked his head back over his shoulder. "He's inside. He'll pull through, but he ain't in no condition to back us." Clete paused and grimaced. "Juan took the whip to him when he was down. Don't know why a man would have a call to go and do something like that."

"I do," Stark said. "It was a message for me."

He calculated swiftly. Trying to round up a posse from Doaksville would take time, and was probably futile anyway. Not many folks would be willing to help, and them that were would likely just get in the way when the lead started flying. He tried to picture Fort Towson from the last time he'd seen it. That had been a good spell back.

"What's the layout at the fort?" he queried.

He listened and watched as Clete described the ruins and drew a crude diagram in the dust. Stark's memory of the place sharpened.

"We'll be sitting targets if we ride straight in," he assessed aloud. "They'll have all the cover." The need for urgency was goading his thoughts like spurs. "It'll take too long to sneak up on them, and even longer if we wait until dark to try." He chewed it over. "We need cover, but we need to go in fast and hard."

"Why not take that mining wagon and a full team, and shove it right down their throats?" Clete suggested.

Stark met his gaze and let a thin smile crease his lips. "A rolling fortress. It's stood up to bullets before. Just might do the trick."

Even with one arm in a sling, Clete was a good hand at getting the mules hitched. With hammer and nails, Stark rigged slots to secure his rifle and shotgun in the bed.

"I'll take the lines," he said once they had the wagon and team out from under the shed. "Can you give me some cover fire with just one hand?"

"One hand's all I need." Clete dropped his gnarled palm to the butt of his monstrous revolver. "Hang on a minute." He disappeared into the barn, emerging a moment later with the oilskin-wrapped Bible from his Pony Express days. "Reckon I better take this along." He slipped it inside his shirt. "I'm ready."

"Then let's roll."

With Clete beside him on the seat, Stark kicked off the brake and put the mules into their traces with a yell and a pop of his whip. For now, his rifle and shotgun were booted next to him. Clete was packing only his Beaumont-Adams. His black leather fighting whip lay coiled at his feet.

Stark kept the mules to a good clip. The wagon bounced joltingly beneath them.

"How many guns you figure we're facing?" Stark asked at length.

Clete's answer was grim. "Better count on a good eight or so, including Juan. Things were kind of confused there for a time, and I didn't get a good count."

"Did you see any lookouts at the fort?"

"They didn't see me; I didn't see them. But you can figure on there being a few of them scattered among them ruins, up close to the trading post. We can't come at them from the back with that creek behind them. It'll be like running into a shooting gallery to take this wagon in there."

"These targets shoot back."

"Pull up here," Clete directed. "Better have a look-see from that ridge yonder. You can view the whole fort from there."

Stark took his field glasses and went forward on foot. He was tempted to take the sporting rifle and look for targets, but sharpshooting would only betray their presence. Shooting gallery or not, the rolling fortress was still their best bet.

On his belly, shielding the lenses with one hand, he surveyed the U-shaped collection of structures below. He could see a handful of men loitering in front of the ramshackle log building, but Juan was not among them. He forced his thoughts away from what might be going on inside the post.

After five minutes he managed to detect movement behind the crumbling wall of one of the outermost structures. He didn't take time looking for other sentries.

Tersely he reported his findings to Clete. The old-timer nodded mutely, then pulled his revolver to check the loads.

Stark took the reins and scrambled over the seat into the bed of the wagon. To remain exposed on the seat was a greenhorn's move. This way he would have some cover from head-on fire. He secured his long guns in the makeshift slots, and stuck the butt of Clete's fighting whip in his belt. He didn't cotton to using it on the hapless mules, but its wicked sting and extra length would make them give their best.

Clete braced himself in a front corner of the bed and drew his pistol "Let's stretch them out," he said.

Feet spread for purchase, Stark jigged the lines and put the mules moving up the steep slope. They mounted its crest, and the fort was spread out below them. The old parade ground, with the hulls of buildings lining either side, made a gauntlet with the trading post the goal at the far end.

Stark popped the reins to get the team moving at a little better clip. He waited until he felt the steepness of the grade adding to their speed, then he shifted all the lines to his left hand. Driving an eight-up team with one hand was fool's work, but so was this wild charge into the teeth of enemy guns.

He plucked the whip from his belt, whirled it once above him to gain velocity, then cracked it over the backs of the mules and cut loose with a wildcat yell. Startled, the animals lunged forward, and the massive wagon went down the slope like an avalanche on wheels.

Stark let the team have its head. Bellowing, and burning the nearest animals with the wicked whip, he fought with tensed legs to stay on his feet. For a pair of gut-wrenching seconds the wagon was actually gaining on the mules, who were pulling for all their worth to escape the whip-wielding demon behind them.

Then they jolted out onto the flat. The first of the ruins flashed past. There was no need for working the reins now. The critters ran flat out up the parade ground, each of them trying to outrace his mate. Wind tore at Stark's face. He bared his teeth into it, yelled again, and sent the whip cracking out.

The left front wheel hit a chuckhole, unseen in the tall grass. The wagon bounced high, threatened to tip over, then came down with a rattling crash. Stark was flung sideways, caught his balance, and had to use both hands on the reins, hauling hard on the right side to straighten the team out.

He glimpsed movement in one of the buildings, and heard the cannon roar of Clete's revolver. A hit or a miss, he couldn't tell. A miracle the old-timer was able to get off a shot at all.

Up ahead a man stepped into view from behind a half-fallen wall, raising a rifle to aim at the oncoming juggernaut. If one mule went down, the whole outfit would go sky-west-and-crooked, Stark thought in that instant. Then Clete extended his pistol over the side of the wagon and dropped the hammer. Recoil flung his arm upwards. Powder smoke was whipped back into Stark's eyes. Incredibly, whether by luck or skill, the bullet drove home. Stark had a single image of the rifleman hurled back off his feet as the wagon thundered past. Clete let out a wordless battle cry.

They roared down on the trading post. Figures were scattering or trying to line their guns. Clete flung lead at them. His shots, and the spectacle of the maddened team bearing down upon them, caused most of their fire to go wild. Still, a bullet sang past Stark's ear.

Coolly one of the hard cases dropped to his knee, propping his gunhand on a bent forearm to aim. But he'd waited too late. Stark saw the horror dawn in his wide-eyed face an instant before he disappeared under the driving hooves of the team. The wagon jolted twice, and his screams were cut off. Stark didn't try to look back.

The log front of the post rushed to meet them. In another few seconds the berserk team would plow full into it. Stark hauled back hard on the left lines, twisting his whole body into the effort, as he loosened up on the right lines.

Stub, the lead mule on the left, responded, veering in that direction, pulling the right lead animal around with him. The whole team turned in a tight arc. The heavy wagon slewed around broadside to the building, rocking up on two of its towering wheels before crashing back to earth. The vehicle came to a jarring halt.

Gunfire sizzled the air. Stark whipped both sets of lines around a corner upright of the bed, snatched his shotgun from its slot. He had a second's view of two men, pistols bared, boiling out of the front door. Clete's Beaumont-Adams boomed, and the lead man was driven against his companion with enough power to send them both sprawling back into the building.

Then Stark had no more time to worry about Clete. One man charged the wagon on foot, six-gun blazing. A couple of others had taken cover behind the closest limestone wall and were winging lead his way.

Stark chose the yahoo on foot first. He was the easiest. The solid load from the shotgun flattened him like he'd been dropped by a mule kick. Stark propped the shotgun barrel on the high rim of the bed and shifted aim toward the fellow hunkered behind a low section separate from the rest of the wall. His head, shoulder and gunarm were visible as he blasted away with his revolver. Plenty of target for buckshot. A final bullet chunked into the side of the wagon as Stark cut loose with the shotgun. The shootist disappeared like a knockdown target in a shooting gallery.

Rifle lead cut a groove next to Stark's arm. The third hombre had better cover. His rifle barrel poked through a fissure in the wall that made a fine gun port. Stark ducked as he fired again, then popped back up and emptied the shotgun at the telltale barrel. A solid load, then buckshot, then another solid slug, tore into the limestone. It was old and weathered, its porous surface decayed by years of wind and rain.

Stark blinked through gunsmoke and saw that the fissure had been replaced by a hole as big as his head. The rifle barrel jerked back out of sight.

Stark delayed an instant, then slapped both hands on the rim of the bed and vaulted from the wagon. He wobbled as he landed, before catching his balance. He raced around the end of the wall, pulling his six-gun as he moved. The wounded rifleman was weaving on his knees, still trying to raise his weapon. Stark fired from the hip—once, twice— and the fellow wilted.

Stark's nerves sang high and shrill, because there was still at least one of the enemy unaccounted for, and he was the most dangerous of all. He sensed movement further back in the ruins, and dropped flat a half-heartbeat before a bullet sliced through the space his skull had just occupied.

Stark snaked through the grass to the lowest point of the wall. He raised up, then ducked back just as quickly because his foe would be waiting for him to reveal himself when he returned fire. In the fractional instant's view that he had, he saw the expected poncho-clad figure framed in an empty window of the adjacent structure.

A revolver bullet chipped limestone and screamed off in a ricochet. Juan didn't have the firepower to blast through walls. And now neither did Stark. His empty shotgun lay back in the wagon where he'd left it.

He waited a pair of seconds then lifted his head again, hoping he'd guessed Juan's next move just like the gaucho had anticipated his a moment before. His guess was a good one. With his position known, Juan was seeking other cover. He disappeared just ahead of Stark's snapped shot. Stark sought some different cover himself.

He hunkered down and chewed things over as he reloaded. Anxiety ate at him. Gunshots from behind him told him Clete was still trading fire with at least one jasper holed up in the building.

This deadly game of stalk and kill between himself and Juan could go on for the rest of the waning day. It needed to be ended.

"Hey, Peacemaker!"

Stark started as Juan's voice echoed from among the ruins. "I hear you!" he shouted back, then shifted positions.

"You crippled my brother! He will always limp now!" Juan's challenging voice rang out. The echoing walls made it impossible to pinpoint his whereabouts.

"Your brother wasn't as *muy hombre* as he thought." Maybe Juan was once again figuring along the same lines as he was, Stark reflected. He let a beat go by, then added, "What about you, gaucho?"

"What are you saying, hombre?"

"You laid the leather to a helpless kid. I been thinking you gauchos ain't so much after all." Stark lifted his voice jeeringly. "Look at you! You're nothing but a backdoor man to a high dollar dance hall queen. She kept you on a leash while she threw herself at me right in front of you! *Gaucho*. What a laugh! A bad joke! I'm wondering if you'd be willing to try what you did to that kid against someone who can fight back."

Juan sputtered with rage. "Show yourself, *gringo,* and we will settle this without *pistolas. Mano a mano!*"

Stark holstered his Colt. The truth in his scathing words had bit deep into the gaucho's fiery pride. Juan wouldn't use a gun now if his life depended on it.

Stark grinned at the thought. He straightened to his feet and strode out into the open.

For a moment he detected no sign of life amidst the pale ruins. His ears rang from the gunfire. Then, over the ringing, he heard another sound, like the blades of a windmill turning ever faster in the rush of a norther.

Juan stepped into view. Spinning over his head, the heavy iron balls all but invisible in their speed, was his bolas.

"Hai, Peacemaker!" he yelled, and hurled the bolas.

The throwing rope had killed two men and probably more. Its iron balls were weighted specially to break the neck and crack the skull of any human it caught. In a blur it spun through the air toward Stark.

Stark's arm moved just as fast as when he'd made his draw against the Konowa Kid. His big bowie knife flashed into view, and he threw it overhand with a single powerful surge of motion. Glinting in the sunlight it cartwheeled to intercept the oncoming bolas. Razor-sharp steel met taut braided leather in mid-flight and severed it cleanly. Two iron balls sailed off in different directions. The third, its power depleted, thumped to the ground and rolled almost to Stark's feet. A section of leather was still attached to it. Stark nudged the heavy sphere aside with a booted toe.

"Works better on old men who don't see it coming," he advised. His tone was contemptuous, but in truth he hadn't been sure if his stunt with the bowie would succeed.

Juan's dissipated hawkish features darkened with feral rage. He pulled his poncho off and flung it savagely aside to free his arms. Then he plucked his coiled bullwhip off his belt and gripped the butt in one big fist. "I hoped it would come to this," he growled.

"So did I," Stark said. Then he unfastened Clete's whip from where he'd wrapped it around his waist before leaving the wagon, and shook it loose.

Juan's eyes widened. "So, you have got a real whip."

"Yeah." Stark made the leather writhe along the ground. "You marked the boy. Now I'll give you a taste of my rawhide."

"No, *gringo,* it is I who will give you a taste, and more. I will not stop even after you are dead!"

With his words he sprang forward, swinging his whip arm in a level arc rather than the overhand blow Stark was expecting. It brought his whip lashing in from the side to wrap itself around Stark's waist like a red-hot serpent. Stark gasped in pain and swung his rawhide overhead to strike in counter.

Before he could complete the move, Juan set himself and hauled back hard on his whip. Stark spun like a top and crashed to the ground as the braided leather unwrapped itself from around him.

He was half stunned, shocked by the sudden and unorthodox style of the gaucho's attack. His gut was on fire. He heard the pound of Juan's feet and knew that in another instant the weighted tip of Juan's lash would be tearing at his flesh. Juan's vow to flay his lifeless body flashed through his mind.

Lying on his side, Stark swung his whip in an unorthodox strike of his own, barely a foot above ground level. He aimed at Juan's charging legs and saw the rawhide coil about both calves. He rolled sideways, yanking on his whip. Juan hit the grass with a startled grunt and Stark's rawhide came free.

Stark scrambled to his feet, but he was no faster than Juan, and it was the gaucho who whirled his leather overhead and struck first. Stark shifted his head like he was slipping a punch. The lead tip tore through fabric and bit into his shoulder. It he hadn't dodged, it would've taken one of his eyes.

Before he could set himself, Juan lashed out again and yet again. He kept the whip moving, using arm and wrist to send that deadly tip at Stark's face, then at his chest, then curling over his shoulders. Stark reeled backwards, but Juan's devilish lash stayed with him. It stung and burned and sliced until the successive pops rang in Stark's ears like a barrage of gunfire. He understood remotely that it had been too long since he'd handled a fighting whip against a man who knew how to use one. Juan bid fair to cut him to pieces. The gaucho was laughing with savage brutal pleasure.

Desperately Stark dodged behind a short section of wall to escape that cutting lash. The leaden pellet struck chips from the soft limestone inches behind him. He heard Juan's angry curse.

Stark's shirt was in tatters, and he was bleeding from a dozen slices. Pain wracked his body. But for the moment he was clear of Juan's reach. He sprang around the other end of the wall and went at the gaucho like an avenging angel, his rawhide cracking overhead. Juan gave a barbaric cry and came to meet him.

Their two black snakes hissed and cracked and cut in a slashing exchange of leather. In seconds, Juan's shirt was torn to ribbons as well, and his arms and torso were marked by angry welts. Stark felt his enemy's weapon bite back, but the old rhythms of slash and cut had returned to him, and he gave as good as he got.

Maybe better. They reeled apart. Juan was a bloody scarecrow. Even his handsome ravaged face had been marked. Stark didn't figure he himself looked much better. Juan seemed ready to fight on to the end, but some saner portion of Stark's mind whispered that this duel could be the death of both of them. And Prudence was still in the merciless clutches of Norene Danner.

Juan tossed his head like a stallion, bared his teeth, and came in again, black snake uncoiling in the air. Stark flipped his lash out in a lazy underhand toss, not looking for speed or even power, just setting a trap. Juan's descending whip met it, lashed about it like one serpent attacking another, and, all in a second, the two whips were tangled tight together. Instantly Stark jerked his own lash taut. His boot stomped down hard on the braided leather, pinning it to the ground. The unexpected tension on Juan's whip yanked the butt of it clean from his sweaty grip.

Juan froze in shock. Reversing the hilt of his own rawhide, Stark leaped forward and clubbed him hard alongside the head. Juan's knees buckled. He still seemed to be staring in stunned disbelief as he crumpled senseless to the grass.

"I said you might get a chance to see if I'd make a good gaucho," Stark rasped.

Panting, he bent toward the fallen man. In a trice he had Juan disarmed and hog-tied with his own whip. There wasn't any time to enjoy his victory or to try to recover from it. He understood with a sense of surprise that only scant minutes had passed since the wild charge in the wagon, and gunfire still barked from back at the trading post.

Limping, Stark legged it out of the ruins. He spotted Clete forted up in the wagon, plugging shots at the building where at least one more of Norene's gunhawks was holed up.

Stark kept the bulk of the wagon between him and the structure as he drew near. "How many?" he hawked.

Clete looked around, saw him, and took a couple of seconds to gape in amazement. Then he gave his head a shake. "Just one," he reported. "No way I could rush him."

"Cover me." Stark palmed his Colt and ripped the little double-action .38 from its hidden holster at the small of his back.

With Clete's hand cannon booming, he rounded the wagon and charged the door, firing both guns, right and left. He threw a hip-twisting kick that splintered wood and flung the panel inward. He burst into the building, glimpsing the chair that had barricaded the door flying across the room under the force of his kick. Then he was swiveling at the waist to fire both guns simultaneously at the hard case spinning toward him from a broken window. The ranny never got off a shot. He jolted back against the wall from the impact of two bullets, and slid to the floor.

In the far corner of the big room a rickety table had been overturned for protection. Brenda and Brian were bound to chairs. Brian looked the worse for wear. His battered face told of a beating.

Prudence was in a chair opposite the pair, covered by a tiny derringer held firmly in the ivory hand of Norene Danner. Prudence had been left unbound, likely so she could sign the papers which had spilled onto the floor when the table had been upended.

As Stark wheeled toward them, Norene Danner gave him a single wild-eyed look, then whirled and plunged toward a rear door.

Prudence came up out of her chair like she'd been pitched by a wild bronc. One trim leg swept in a smooth arc that caught Norene's ankle and threw her face-first onto the dusty floor, to land with an unladylike grunt. Prudence's other foot flicked out, and the derringer skittered away.

"No you don't, you hussy!" Prudence snapped with heartfelt satisfaction.

"I got that she-cat covered!" Clete's voice barked from the front doorway.

Stark holstered both guns and covered the distance between him and Prudence in two long strides. She met him halfway. Tears and happiness were on her face, and relief gripped Stark's heart. Before he quite knew how it happened, she was in his arms and he was hugging her slender form to him. He felt her arms tighten around him in response. She was all supple softness and strength.

He loosened his hold, and she drew back in the circle of his arms. Her face was uplifted, her lips parted. Without thought Stark bent toward her. Her eyes slid closed expectantly.

Some distant realization of what he was about to do stirred in Stark. He stiffened. In the same instant Prudence went rigid against him. Her eyes popped open and gazed up at him with what was almost fear. Stark reckoned his eyes looked about the same way.

Hastily he released her and stepped back.

Her features were more flushed than he'd ever seen them. And more beautiful. He swallowed hard. Behind Prudence, Norene Danner stirred and muttered softly.

Stark nodded weakly in that direction. "Where'd you learn how to do that?"

Prudence gave him a shaky grin. "I've picked up a few useful things from spending time with you," she said.

Chapter Nineteen

U.S. Deputy Marshal Chris Madsen propped his shoulders against the wall in the kitchen of the B&B, and used a forefinger to tip his hat back. He shook his head in wonder. "I made it here as quick as I could when I got your message, Jim. Guess I still missed all the fun. That's quite a tale. Sounds like the Widow Danner was bound and determined to get you to sign those papers, Miss Prudence. Course, once she did, you and the Langton kids would've been finished."

Prudence nodded. She sat across the table from Stark. Their hands, apparently by accident, had come to rest only inches apart on the tabletop. Neither seemed aware of it.

"We all knew what would happen if we signed," she said to the lawman. "That's why none of us would consent. Even when she had her thugs beat Brian, Brenda and I knew we couldn't give in to her demands." She paled a little at the memories. "I hate to think what she would've come up with next to force us to put our names on those papers.''

So did Stark. He was stiff and sore, and he figured he'd be feeling the touch of Juan's whip in his nightmares even after the actual welts had healed. Prudence's likely fate if he and Clete had taken much longer in busting things up would also be playing a part of his midnight hauntings.

''We've got the Konowa Kid, the big gaucho and that devil of a woman locked up safe and sound over to the local hoosegow.'' Madsen let a slight grin show under his mustache. ''Reckon the locals will be looking for a new lawman. Ain't seen hide nor hair of Marshal Bailey since we brought them in.''

''They'll be prosecuted of course.'' Prudence made it a statement.

Madsen nodded. ''That's a safe bet, for sure. You've uncovered enough evidence hereabouts to have the U.S. marshal's office interested for quite a spell. That two-bit gunfighter is already spilling his guts on everything he knows. And from the way the widow and the gaucho were bad-mouthing each other, I'd be surprised if they don't each end up testifying against one another. Between them and the couple of hard cases Stark and that old codger left alive at the fort, we shouldn't have any trouble finding plenty of charges to bring.''

''I could think of a few,'' Prudence said in a low tone that made Stark glance at her.

She didn't meet his gaze. ''I'll open the probate as soon as possible, she went on quickly. ''I wouldn't anticipate problems with it. The company should be operating again before too long.''

Like Stark, the other menfolk of the B&B were recovering from the hardships they'd undergone. Brian was up and about. Brenda was nursing the other two. Clete had complained that she was neglecting him in favor of Josh.

The old mule skinner didn't seem too upset about it, however.

"Well, I've still got to go see about transporting the widow and her sorry crew back to McAlister," Madsen announced, straightening away from the wall. "I better get to it."

"Watch out for her, Chris," Stark warned only half jokingly. "She's dangerous as a stepped-on scorpion, and, believe me, her sting ain't her only weapon." He avoided looking at Prudence as he spoke.

Madsen grinned. "Don't worry, cowboy. She's got me plumb scared." He eyed them both shrewdly. "You two stay out of trouble, you hear?"

Stark and Prudence drew their hands a little further apart.

Madsen's grin widened. "So long."

They saw him out, then Prudence turned and looked up at Stark. She cocked her head quizzically. "Any regrets, cowboy?"

Stark gave it some thought. "Nope. But the next time I work for you, I want it clear who should be in charge."

Prudence smiled demurely. "Oh," she said, "There's no question about that."